First Time

Elite Escorts 4

Lynn Burke

First Time

I'm Elite Escort's shibari master—but I'm no sadist. I love sending a client flying, finding comfort in my ropes. Some view my form of play as an act of domination, but I see it as a way to offer an escape.

Childhood trauma honed my intuition, making me notice what others easily miss.

When a curvy sub, leashed and cowering behind a man playing Dom, visit the club I frequent, my protective instincts kick in.

Faced with an opportunity to reveal to Becky what a real D/s relationship is supposed to look like, I take on the challenge. I observe more while binding her in my ropes— bruises she attempts to hide behind her lowered head and long hair.

She's a battered and broken spirit worn down by years of abuse—the same as my mom had been. I refuse to let her meet the same fate, but for the first time, it's my hands that are tied.

While I long to help Becky break free, it's up to her to find the courage to take control—before it's too late.

Trigger warnings: Domestic, Verbal, Sexual, & Physical Abuse (not by MMC), Violence

Chapter 1

Daniel

My client for the night hung upright from the ring affixed to her ceiling, my ropes crossing her torso with intricate knots that had taken me over an hour to tie. I'd bent her legs back and bound her heels to her thighs with a frog tie, and her hands clasped behind her neck were also secured in place. Simple brushes of my fingertips over her pale, smooth skin had her hovering near euphoria long before I'd hefted her body into the air.

Suspended upright, she swung gently and in silence except for her heightened breaths, the top of her head level with my chin. Her long, blonde hair hung down her back like a golden waterfall, caressing her curved spine and the globes of her bare, rounded ass.

I stepped between her spread knees, my leather pants keeping my flaccid cock from pressing into her ass crack. The scent of expensive perfume lingered after her long day at work beneath hot cameras and her producer's intense stare.

"Color, Bunny?" I murmured against her ear.

"Green," she replied, barely more than a needy whisper.

She'd shared about her day on set when I'd first arrived for our scene, how the stress had taken her to the limit of her ability to perform. Thus, her reason for calling Elite Escorts, desperate for a last-minute appointment with their shibari master.

Me.

Daniel Cooney, a six-foot-five wall of muscled Dom who intimidated the hell out of clients until I allowed them to get to know me better. Sitting down and explaining the power dynamic between dominants and submissives to new customers always brought calm to their nervous tension when they realized my insides didn't match my exterior.

And when they gave consent for me to use bondage to set them free?

Fucking magic emanated from my caring hands and concentrated attention fixed solely on helping them find release.

"Are you ready to come for me?" My hot breath on her earlobe sent a tremor through her.

"Yes, Sir," she moaned her response, free in a way she never could be at a BDSM club due to her TV personality.

Reaching around her body, I found her folds slick with arousal but took care to not dip into her heat.

Bunny's limits included penetration of anything outside of toys. She didn't allow kissing on any part of her body either. No teeth. No tongue. But I knew how to use my hands and all ten fingers to the best of my ability when it came to rigging clients and sending their minds into oblivion.

The dildo I'd chosen for her that night had girth and length outside the norm, but she loved when I used it on her needy pussy. The silicone made a squelching noise as I slid it deep inside her core.

Bunny released a guttural groan, her head tipping back against my shoulder as I slowly fucked her with the toy. "So good, Sir," she panted, pliant in my arms.

I hummed my approval over her pleasure, wishing my own body found some sense of fulfillment outside of a job well done.

"Let go for me, Bunny." I leaned down to press my cheek against hers. She shivered beneath my fingertips trailing down her bare torso. Goose bumps rose in my touch's wake between cords of rope. I dipped over her pubis, and she whimpered, shifting against my chest as I caressed over her prominent clit. "That's it," I murmured, peering down over her harnessed chest to watch my fingers strum her hardened nub.

Her breaths grew frantic, gasped inhales. Shudders rippled over her. Her cheek grew clammy against mine as sweat rose to coat her body.

I fucked her with the dildo and rubbed over her clit with firm pressure, my pride getting off on how she gave over to her body's need for release.

"Come all over my hand, Bunny."

She cried out, her body tensing and then trembling through orgasm.

"Such a good girl," I crooned, nuzzling against her ear.

Wetness dripped onto the hardwood floor of her bedroom, the musky sweetness of her cum filling my nose.

"You soaked me, Bunny. Fuck." I groaned along with her, taking pleasure in her release even though no arousal slid through my blood. She hung in rapture while I stood in reality, unfulfilled and left wanting, my dick still limp inside my leathers.

Quietness settled over us, and I slowly pulled the toy from her pussy. "Okay?" I asked quietly, soothing her hip with a gentle caress.

"Yes, Sir." Her breathless tone made me smile as satisfaction swelled up inside my chest.

Twenty minutes later, I sat against her headboard, cradling my favorite client's slight form in my arms. She'd had a bottle of water to drink, but I continued to hold her as she came down, her body a limp noodle on my lap.

"I can't ever love a man," she told me, gazing up from where her head rested in the crook of my arm, "but if I could, it would be you."

"You don't want to love me," I said with a chuckle, affection for her making me want to kiss her on the nose. "I'm not capable of giving it physically in return."

"Are you asexual?"

I studied her upturned face and big blue eyes for a few minutes, not surprised by her bluntness. Fuck knew we'd had hours of talks amassed after all the scenes we'd done together over the nine months I'd been with Elite. She hadn't ever asked about my lack of arousal while binding her before.

"No," I finally answered. "I get horny, but not very often. If clients want to be fucked, I have little blue pills. I've just...never felt a connection with anyone, a desire to be intimate emotionally. For a while, I wondered if I might be demisexual, but I experienced insta-lust a time or two when I was younger." Shrugging, I snuggled her closer. "I'll be honest though, if I could fall in love, it would be with you too."

She snorted with laughter. "Every warm-blooded male and queer female between puberty and death would say the same to my face given the chance."

Bunny didn't lie. She had the looks and body of a goddess along with more money than her grandchildren's grandchildren could spend in their lifetime. Her laughter was infectious. Her smile dazzling. Her kindness worthy of sainthood.

"Maybe," I said, "but you know I don't give a rat's ass about your pretty face and riches. I would fall for you because you submit so easily for me. You find your release every time I bind you in my ropes. The level of trust you give me is staggering..." My voice trailed off as a slight ache radiated through my chest.

"So you're saying I'm everything you could ever want, but there's no spark. No connection." She didn't sound put out, simply matter-of-fact.

"Unfortunately, you're spot on," I agreed.

Her sweet smile sent warmth through me but from shared friendship rather than desire. "You deserve to find the perfect partner, Daniel." Bunny caressed my closely-clipped beard. "You're a beautiful soul. Protective and sensitive. Any woman would be lucky to have you by their side and in their bed."

"Most women see my intimidating size and run the other way," I muttered what I found to be true more often than not whenever I went out with my friends. Some didn't —but those women tended to be dick-hungry and only wanted what I packed between my thighs. Hookups like that turned me off and held no sway over my cock, so what was the point?

"Someday, you're going to find the love of your life who fits your kinky lifestyle to a T, and I'll be here pouting over losing my Sir—but I'll be happy for you."

Most women who liked being tied up expected and enjoyed pain with their pleasure, something I refused to give. Even when payment was offered in exchange. I'd spent my childhood watching my father, who thought roughing up my mom made him a real man.

The fucker.

The last thing I would ever do while breath lingered in my lungs was lay a hand on a woman to inflict harm of any sort.

"Time for me to go, Bunny," I murmured and rubbed my cheek against her soft hair, needing to shut down thoughts of the past.

Roused memories never left me in a good place, and I preferred to avoid them as well as not bring them into any conversation. No one but the people from my childhood and law enforcement back in Ohio knew what had happened when I was thirteen—and I planned to keep it that way. A half hour later, I sat in my SUV heading home and feeling sorry for myself. And not for the first time after sceneing with a paying customer.

A lot of my fellow escorts who worked for Elite had found their soulmates, the women that completed them. Blake with Wren. Reid and Jessie. The summer before, Jarod had fallen for Christine. She owned his soul, and he'd captured her adoration and trust. They had survived a suicide bomber and had been buried beneath rubble for hours, and their resulting happiness brought a level of jealousy I'd never felt before. The way her gaze lingered on him and the look of pure love and acceptance in her eyes hit me every time.

To find a woman like that would be pure bliss.

Micah, Elite's owner and one of my best friends, had replaced all three of his former employees, but I wondered if I would be so lucky to find the love of a lifetime as they had. If and when such an occurrence took place, Micah would be pissed. Happy for me like Bunny, but upset at losing yet another of his escorts.

I wasn't actively seeking, wasn't turned off by the thought of a ball and chain—quite the opposite. But finding someone who would fit me and my kinks, a submissive into bondage that would give me her trust to not hurt her? Not an easy feat. Chantelle's, an exclusive BDSM club in downtown Boston, offered one of the few smorgasbords for people in the lifestyle, and I visited every Friday night when I wasn't on the clock for Elite.

But I'd yet to run into a woman I felt drawn to, one who loved my ropes as much as I did without the pain play often associated with being bound.

A woman to help me prove to the world that a boy didn't always grow up to be like his bastard father.

Chapter 2

Becky

A nip lingered in the air even though spring approached, so I decided to make chicken soup for dinner. It was one of Stephen's favorites.

As always when his workday neared its end, my insides clenched, and my mind flitted from one thought to the next. Would he enter the house red-faced from anger as he'd been doing lately? Maybe he'd had a better day and would lean in to kiss me. Anxiety would probably have his shoulders heightened, and I would walk on eggshells, trying to stay out of his way until we crawled into bed.

We'd been together since high school. Sweethearts once upon a time, but the daily grind of life and paying bills had weighed on our relationship over the years.

Breathing slowly, I chopped onions and carrots into perfect-sized chunks. Potatoes instead of rice or noodles, because it was what Stephen preferred, went into the home-made broth next. Some thyme and sage...a bit of chopped garlic.

The scent of comfort and warmth rose up my nose, and

I closed my eyes, smiling from finding pleasure in the small things.

Cooking had become my meditation, how I relaxed my mind and quieted my thoughts toward the aspiration of a more pleasant future rather than feeling sorry for myself.

I had to believe that Stephen and I could get back to where we used to be—loving and kind to one another. Hope had become the lifeline I clung to. What other choice did I have? My parents were both gone. I had no siblings, nor did I have the education or means to support myself.

Stephen loved me. I just had to help him through his latest unsettled time so he could remember how to find happiness in our relationship.

I'd baked homemade bread earlier in the day and took my time cutting it into even slices. Butter sat on a small dish on the counter, room temperature, exactly as Stephen liked for easy spreading. I dished up a small bowl of strawberry jam to go with it too.

The front door opened, sending adrenaline rushing through me—partly excitement to see him and an equal measure of trepidation over his mood.

"I'm in the kitchen!" I called out to Stephen since he liked to know where I was at all times in the house.

Ever since he'd started to upload videos of us to a porn website, he'd become overly protective. Possessive. As though men who enjoyed watching the stuff he did to an overweight woman like me would turn them obsessed to the point they would attempt to kidnap me. He'd even bought extra deadbolts to keep anyone from stealing me away. I was his perfect pain whore who helped ease his tension when he got riled up.

But I hated his newfound kink. He'd taken it to the extreme in attempts to turn me on.

I never climaxed. Ever. Not even back when we were young. He called me broken but loved me anyway. I'd been lucky to have such a man.

These days?

"Becky—

I flinched before I could stop it as Stephen strode into the kitchen, work boots trailing slush from last night's snowstorm across the vinyl tile I'd scrubbed an hour earlier.

"—get me a beer, would ya?"

"I just mopped the floor," I stated quietly while opening the fridge.

"*I just mopped the floor,*" he mocked with a high tone while tossing his lunch box onto the counter. "You should see the shit I had to take care of down at the shop today. Davis spilled a quart of oil—fucking *motor* oil—and didn't have time to clean it up. Guess who got volunteered for the job?"

I tuned out Stephen's complaints, the same as always, and retrieved dishes to set the table. Murmuring agreements and the occasional nod allowed him to think, and I listened intently as he expected me to.

"I want to leave by seven. Can you hurry your ass along to be ready on time for a change?"

Shit.

My hand trembled as I set a spoon atop the napkin beside his bowl. I'd missed whatever he'd been talking about. "Um...yes?"

Snickering, he walked past me and swatted my ass —hard.

I bit back my grimace, not wanting to turn him on and end up in the dungeon he'd built for us—*him*—in our basement.

"Fuck, I love how squishy you are under my hand," he claimed before slapping me again.

A soft squeak escaped me, and he grabbed hold of my flesh, resting his chin on my shoulder. Easily done as he wasn't much taller than me, but I had a good seventy pounds on his thin frame. Hot breath on my ear sent a shiver down my spine. "I don't know how I got so fucking lucky."

Warmth flooded my chest, and I smiled, ready to curl up his arms.

"That woman from the BDSM club claimed I filled out the entry form two months ago. Must have been drunk off my ass." Snorting, Stephen released my ass and moved toward the sink.

Slowly, I returned to setting the table, deciding to pay attention for a change since I'd misread what I'd thought had been a nice compliment.

Water ran behind me as he washed up. "She contacted me through the site I uploaded our latest video to—the one where I caned your ass and emptied my balls all over your back."

His words caused me to wince. The memory of that night made me want to vomit.

He'd been out of control. Drunk. Angry at his boss at the car shop for something or another.

At least he hadn't broken my skin.

"A fucking free pass to a shibari class and access to the entire place for the night!" He laughed. "Can you imagine? It's like the number one exclusive club in Boston. Last I'd heard, the owner went to an invite-only policy because too many people tried to join. Fuck."

I put the pieces of the puzzle my ears had missed

together. He'd won a pass to a BDSM club in Boston and planned on dragging me along with him to check it out.

Ever since he'd found kink porn, Stephen had gone down a road I wasn't comfortable with. He'd started with restraints, and I'd agreed because I was willing to play as long as it made him happy and loving. Cuffs hadn't made me wet for him, so he'd turned to rope. Then chains. Neither encouraged my body to produce moisture to ease penetration.

Then a flogger arrived in a discrete box.

A paddle.

A whip.

Finally, a cane.

He'd studied websites and claimed to educate himself on how to be a proper Dom.

I'd found the guts to tell him pain didn't give me any pleasure and that I would prefer other things in the bedroom. That paddle had bruised my backside beneath his swings. I hadn't been able to sit for five days because I'd dared to question his leadership.

"I-I'd rather not go," I managed to find my voice, knowing honesty might land me strapped down to a table and crying before night's end.

"Tough shit." His tone didn't allow for argument. "You'll wear that long black coat in public and nothing else for when we walk through the club's door."

My stomach churned, threatening to spew bile up my throat. "Stephen—"

"I don't want to hear it, Becky!" he shouted, glowering at me, dark eyes glinting. Unyielding. "Do you know how hard it is to get into a club like this? The amount of money it costs for a fucking membership? Tens of thousands! If you think for one second that I'm going to give up this chance of a lifetime because you're self-conscious, you're delusional. We're going—and I *will* find something there that will turn your frigid body on."

I swallowed hard, trying not to spill the soup while dishing it up.

We settled at the table without another word. I knew better than to question after he laid the law down.

Stuck.

That was what I was. I stared at my soup, appetite voracious when a normal woman wouldn't be able to stand the thought of food while fighting back tears.

I'd been with Stephen for years. We'd grown up together. He'd been one of the few who hadn't bullied me for my plump size all through our childhood. Unfortunately, I'd never thinned out while growing taller. At five-foot-eight, I shouldn't have weighed almost double what a woman my size ought to. But Stephen liked my curves, grabbed them all the time, and told me how he enjoyed watching my fatty flesh ripple while he pounded into me.

I wished I was so easily turned on.

Sighing, I dipped myself another bowlful.

"Hurry it up," Stephen said, pushing aside his half-finished soup and scooting back his chair. "I want you showered and shaved. Leave the pussy hair though—just trim it up a bit. Can't have you looking like a slob on my leash."

Heat rushed to my face, and I bowed my head over my dinner, eyes closing.

"What? Did you think I was going to hold your hand and lead you around like a lover? You're going as my sub tonight. Demure and quiet until I demand your tears."

Did he expect to scene in front of other people? I opened my mouth to argue, but his next words snapped my jaw shut.

"Chantelle's." He chuckled while bending down to untie his work boots. "I'm so fucking lucky."

Chantelle's.

My cousin's BDSM club...

I stilled, a spoonful of chicken and potatoes near my mouth, not sure what to think or how to feel. I hadn't spoken to my cousin in months, thanks to Stephen taking control over my cell and forbidding me to talk to anyone outside my work at the coffee shop. I knew she'd been into kinky stuff for years, and she'd told me about the club she'd created that allowed her to be free to explore her lifestyle—and get paid to invite others into her space.

Stephen wanted to parade me around her place on a leash. Naked. Doing so would make him happy, and maybe he was right in thinking we might find something that would fix my broken body.

He didn't know my cousin's first name was actually Amber...was the supposed giveaway he'd won *her* doing in order to see me again? Or had Stephen somehow gotten a free pass for the night through a contest he didn't remember entering?

He tossed his boot toward the foyer, and it landed with a heavy thump near the closet door. "I can't wait to show all those Doms what an obedient little slut you are." Stephen barked a laugh, his murky brown eyes turning my way. "Okay, not *little*, but you do obey me. Cry for me when I tell you to. Every guy in that club is going to be jealous of me. Envy me."

I highly doubted Stephen's words, but whatever stroked his ego and made him tolerable—

"Put down your spoon and get over here." He unzipped his work jeans, lifted his hips, and shoved them down his thighs. "Be a good slut and suck my cock. Get me off so I don't blow my load like a goddamned teenager seconds after walking into Chantelle's tonight. I can't fucking wait."

As though my knees knew their place, they didn't complain when I knelt where told. Stephen needed to shower, but I ignored the musk from his long day at work and set my focus on pleasing him.

After release, he always offered a small cuddle and words of praise.

I lived for those moments because they took me back to the way things used to be and gave me hope that we could find happiness like that again. And if nothing else, at least I would get to see my cousin for the first time in too long.

Chapter 3

Daniel

Friday night found me heading downtown to the club as usual. I hadn't even shrugged off my coat inside the entryway when Chantelle herself opened the door to her office on my left and motioned me in.

My brow raised, and I crossed the reception area, entering her domain. Nude paintings lined three of the walls of her office, large windows overlooking Boston's skyline covering the fourth.

"Have a seat, Master Cooney." She settled behind her desk, and I sat on the leather chair facing her after slipping my jacket off my shoulders. "Master Lamond can't make it tonight, so I need to you fill in."

My lifted brow furrowed. I'd done a couple of demonstrations for Chantelle but had no interest in actual classes. "I don't teach."

She peered at me over the wide oak desk, hazel eyes flashing. "You're the best shibari master I've ever met."

"And you've also said I scare the shit out of a lot of your patrons who want to be tied up. Hell, I've seen their grimaces myself." Occasionally, I got to play with a brave soul. It was what kept me walking through Chantelle's door every week.

Her Botox-puffed lips lifted in a Cheshire cat smile. "You look like a badass Dom but you've got a gooey center."

She spoke the truth, but I still frowned. Few knew me in the way Chantelle did. She, like all my other acquaintances in Boston, wasn't aware of how I'd ended up living with my grandpop. I had, however, told her the shorter version of what led me to enjoy bondage.

"Look." She leaned forward, elbows on her desk, hands clasped in front of her. "I need this favor."

I eyed her, hoping to catch a glint in her eyes, some sort of tell since I got the sense she was up to something, but the woman had a face of stone. "You have employees on payroll for this shit. Why me?"

Chantelle's gaze bore into me, and I fought not to shift beneath her Domme stare that I'd seen intimidate more people than even I did. "There's a couple who won a two-night freebie pass to the shibari class, and I can't cancel."

Unease slithered down my spine, but I didn't twitch beneath her scrutiny. "Chantelle doesn't do giveaways," I reminded her.

"Do you trust me?"

"Yes," I didn't hesitate to answer. Chantelle was a ruthless businesswoman and honest to a fault. Hanging out in her club was the highlight of my week after the day job in communications—especially when Elite didn't have any clients lined up for me and I needed an ego boost outlet and might get lucky.

"Do you trust my ability to read people?" she asked.

"I've never met a dominant as intuitive as you." Fucking truth, right there.

"Then do this for me." A rare pleading note rang in her voice. Desperation was something I haven't ever seen in Chantelle.

What plan did she have up her sleeve?

I eyed her for a few more moments of silence, but a conclusion over whatever she played escaped me. "I'll need a sub," I offered an excuse instead.

"Ask for a volunteer from the audience."

"Yeah, right." I chuckled. "No one has offered themselves willingly to me like that since I joined here last winter. I've only gotten to string people up because of your recommendation or prodding."

"Or because a sub gave you a chance to sit and talk with them before sceneing, and they learned you aren't an abusive asshole—I know." That damn smile appeared on her lips again. "I wouldn't ask this of you if I didn't think you could do it."

A sigh heaved my shoulders, a frown once more furrowing my brow. "I've never taught a class before. What the hell am I supposed to say or do?"

Chantelle sat back in her chair and riffled through some papers. "Demonstrate a few of the basics. Wing it."

"Wing it," I echoed while scowling.

"Yes." Her hazel-eyed gaze pierced me where I sat in my chair. "Once a volunteer is in front of you, use your judgment. You, too, are an intuitive dominant, Daniel. One of the best I've ever seen."

Pride swarmed in my chest at her words—but she *was* aware of how I'd survived my early years in Boston.

I dipped my head. "Thank you—and I'll do it. But if anyone demands their money back because I was a total failure, I'm not responsible."

She smiled. "I trust you."

Those words from a woman, let alone a dominant like Chantelle, roused satisfaction deep inside me. I'd striven to be a better man than my father. Had climbed from the ashes and would continue to prove to the world that a man could rise above his circumstances.

"I'm assuming you've had the participants fill out medical history forms for circulation problems, aches, and pains?" I asked, not about to go into leading people who hadn't been properly vetted. Not that Chantelle would ever allow such a thing to happen in her club, but since I was in charge...

"Of course."

"No mobility issues for anyone taking the class? Bending, those sorts of things?"

Chantelle's eyes gleamed as though pleased by my consideration over those who would be beneath my care. "There is a blonde woman with some minor health issues, but I spoke with her about not volunteering."

I exhaled a huge breath and nodded, resigned to complete the favor Chantelle had asked of me.

A few minutes later, I exited her office, suspicion still a live wire in the back of my mind. The woman planned something, and the thought of her devious, controlling nature made me wary as fuck even though I towered over her five-foot-nine height.

After dropping my coat and shirt off in the men's locker/shower room, I entered the lounge to find the dimmed area already packed. Every stool at the bar was occupied, and the groupings of chairs and couches scattered around the room held parties in full-on fun mode.

A sensual, erotic feast for all the senses.

Naked flesh of all colors. Sloppy, tear-inducing blow jobs. Asses being tanned—and fucked—in darker corners.

Arousing low groans and whimpers rose above the soft music drifting down from overhead speakers.

I scanned over the buffet of sex, my body buzzing. While I hadn't hoped or even planned to scene that evening, my blood thrummed with awareness...a sixth sense of expectation.

From Chantelle's invite to teach?

No. The underlying itchiness in my feet and hands had prompted my drive to the club but had grown more intense than the usual prodding on a Friday night.

So what was it? What about the room drew on my awareness and tempted my cock to tingle with anticipation? Arousal stirred in my blood, and I needed to find out why —*who*—had caused an awakening in me I hadn't felt in months.

A smaller Dom on my left caught my gaze. He watched a couple in the middle of a spanking scene. His unimpressive hard-on ridged the front of his low-quality leather pants hugging thin legs. A single rose tattoo inked his upper arm. Hand in a fist, he held tight to a leash.

My gaze slid to the submissive behind him.

Voluptuous, plump flesh...wide hips swelled and led down to thick thighs. Her body would be mouthwatering bound up in my ropes.

Fuck. I rubbed a hand over my scruffy jawline.

Naked and trembling, she stood with her head dipped low, dark hair hiding her face. Huge breasts, nipples plump and soft—

Soft.

The submissive didn't find the atmosphere arousing. She cowered behind her Dom.

Instincts flickered to life in my brain, and I continued to

study him and his sub as he lead her onto the next pairing getting their exhibition kink on.

The sweet, leashed woman was insecure and uncomfortable as fuck with shuffling feet, and her Dom didn't give a shit about her desires. Not once did he glance back to see why she lagged. He simply jerked on the tether between them like she was nothing more than a dog he demanded to heel at his command.

My jaw clenched along with my guts as I stepped off to the side in the shadows. I watched as he led her in a circle around the room pausing on occasion to take in the various scenes. They drew near to where I'd hidden in the shadows, and I forced myself to keep my gaze on her rather than the prick leading her around like she was simply a toy, a plaything, instead of a flesh-and-blood human with feelings.

He drew her forward to the ménage scene on the couch to my left. "How about this?" the wiry asshole asked her with a chuckle. "Double penetration. Two cocks shoved so far up your dry cunt you can't remember your name?"

The woman shook, her hands sneaking down to cover the trimmed thatch of black hair hiding her pussy.

My fist itched to break the dude's nose, the first hint of violence I'd felt since the night I'd—

"Well?" the asshole asked, yanking on her lead rope when she didn't answer. His action kept me in the present. "Does this turn that frigid body of yours on?"

Mother. Fucker. My fists clenched.

The dark-haired woman lifted her head slightly but quickly lowered her gaze once more. "N-no, Sir," she whispered.

"Goddamnit, Becky." The wannabe Dom moved away with fast, annoyed steps, pulling her behind him harshly enough that she stumbled in her haste to keep up. "The fuck is wrong with you?"

Her round ass swayed, all that supple flesh teasing me. Blood rushed to my dick, and I growled at the damn thing.

Now you want to get all excited and play? With a woman who's leashed to another man?

"Fuck." Tearing my gaze off the submissive's lush backside, I strode across the lounge, needing space. Heavy footfalls didn't lessen my anger, and neither did the curses spewing through my head as I slammed through the guarded door leading to the private rooms.

Thick carpet muffled my feet, the sudden silence of the door-lined hall intensifying my lust to hiss and howl like a pissed-off animal. It had been years since my violent streak reared its ugly head, but if that fucker and his woman were taking the bondage class, I was in deep shit.

"Not my monkey, not my circus," I muttered while pushing open the door to the room Chantelle had told me she'd prepared for the class.

Adrenaline raced through my bloodstream, but my hands held steady while rifling through the supplies that had been laid out for the class on the dais. Trying to focus on the task ahead of me, I set up stations for the couples who would be in attendance. Two chairs each. A mat should they wish to sit on the chair. Various lengths of cotton rope.

I returned to the front of the room and created few basic ties with hemp instead of the cheaper material the patrons would use, making quick work of them in practice I didn't need. Going through the motions didn't lessen my aggravation as quickly as I'd hoped for.

The familiar feel of hemp in my hands helped me focus, eventually slowing my heart rate.

I positioned a seat on stage with me at a side angle from where my small audience would sit so my volunteer wouldn't need to face them.

I snorted. I highly doubted I'd get away without having to talk someone into sitting on the chair while their spouse or partner watched me tie them up.

"Hopefully, one of the newer Doms won't mind sharing for an hour," I muttered to myself.

Or, maybe Becky and Dom Wannabe will be in the class, and you can ask her to join you on stage. Show her how a real Dom treats their submissive.

I shook my head.

"Not. Getting. Involved."

Chapter 4

Becky

A young woman had greeted us at the door and given us a tour of Chantelle's. Stephen had told me to remove my coat in the women's locker area, and trembling, I'd done as told, embarrassed by my nakedness.

My cousin hadn't appeared, furthering my questioning of how and why we'd ended up in her club. I hadn't been comfortable with the idea of Stephen and her meeting. Without a doubt, he would expect Chantelle to give us free access, considering I was family. But my hands were tied.

Thankfully, not literally.

Tears pricked at my eyelids, but I refused to cry in front of the members of the packed lounge, even though other subs wore the same amount of clothing I did. I had hoped like crazy that something—anything, pain included —we would see at the kink club would finally make me bloom into a normal woman with a healthy sexual appetite.

Not a single twinge of arousal rose between my thighs from the scenes surrounding us. Blow jobs. Masturbation.

Anal sex. The spanking, I couldn't even stand to hear since I'd learned from too much experience that wasn't my thing.

That fact had never stopped Stephen from trying to turn me on, though.

Stephen paused beside two men taking a blonde woman at the same time. I cringed at the idea of a threesome, knowing that no man but Stephen would ever be turned on by the sight of my *extra*. As usual, his crude remarks burned my cheeks, and I clenched my eyes shut as he announced to all within hearing distance that I was frigid and unable to perform sexually. Thank God for lube, otherwise, I would be in pain more often than not.

A whisper of...*something* slid over my skin, releasing some of the tension knotting my neck and shoulders.

Layers of scents clouded the room, but a waft of spicy citrus flitted past my nose, and I lifted my head, breathing deeply. A strange tingle stirred between my thighs. I'd never smelled anything so delicious.

A quick glance around didn't reveal which man wore the cologne, but a wide-shouldered giant moved across the lounge, russet hair mussed, his tight ass encased in what looked like worn, supple black leather. Heat rushed through my body at the sight of him, and I shifted on my feet, lips parting. Every step landed with confidence. Every stride flexed his fine backside.

I tore my gaze off of him and returned my attention to the floor.

Jealousy was one of Stephen's character flaws, and I knew better than to get caught staring at another man. It would earn me at least an hour under his flogger.

Digging my short nails into my palms, I followed along behind Stephen, humiliated by my nakedness he want to show off. He took pride in how I appeared even though he sometimes teased me for eating too much. He got off on uploading the videos he made of us together onto that site I refused to visit.

But doing those things made him happy. Smile. Sometimes they even brought a return of his gentleness and kisses that reminded me of a better time.

My limbs twitched when we finally left the lounge and headed back through a hallway lined with doors. I kept my focus on the navy carpet beneath my bare feet and Stephen's tug on my collar if I fell behind.

We entered a room, and the lack of sexual sounds and scents enticed me to lift my head for a peek around. A handful of other couples mingled in apparent stations set up for each of them, their quiet murmurs loud in the stillness as Stephen led me farther into the room.

"Good evening," a deep voice rumbled, hushing the others in attendance and drawing my focus to the dais in front of us. The redheaded giant I'd seen walking away from us loomed on stage, his dark-eyed gaze roaming across the couples. His front proved as equally alluring as his backside. Wide shoulders rippled with muscle. Prominent pectorals. Ridges down his abdomen...a red happy trail disappeared into leather pants that cupped his groin like a lover's touch.

I swallowed hard, glancing over his thick thighs, muscular calves, and black boots.

He was perfection...a truly magnificent specimen of a man that acted like a magnet to my body. I wanted to step forward. Feel his eyes on me. His touch. Hell, just hearing his voice—

"I am Master Cooney, and I'm the shibari master who is teaching class tonight in place of Master Lamond." His low tone slid like silk over my ears and pebbled my skin.

That tingle I'd felt in the lounge returned with a bit more force, and I chewed on the inside of my lip trying to figure it out even as my pulse heightened.

His gaze flitted over the crowd, snagging on Stephen as he welcomed us. A frown flitted over his brow before he moved on to the next couple without glancing my way, as though I was nothing more than a lowly sub on a leash, unworthy of his attention.

Eyes stinging, I lowered my head.

Master Cooney continued speaking, but I didn't listen. Although his dismissal of my presence hurt, my body still longed to get closer to him. My feet grew restless, every inch of my skin prickling with awareness regardless of his intimidating size. Like Stephen, the man was a Dom. And the size of his hands? His spankings probably hurt like hell.

A shiver slid down my spine. I did *not* want to find out if that was the case or not.

Stephen tugged on my lead rope, his hand on my lower back pushing me forward fast enough I stumbled. "My Becky will scene with you."

"Wha—"

"Don't you dare embarrass me," Stephen hissed against my ear, unfastening the lead rope from the collar he'd bought to properly parade me around the kink club. "Get your lush ass up there and obey the man."

Open-mouthed, I stared at Stephen, fighting for clarity of what I'd missed. Volunteer. Scene with another Dom. Had Stephen lost his mind? Forgotten his jealousy—it seemed his desire to humiliate me tonight knew no bounds.

He pinched my ass, and I flinched, biting my tongue to keep from squealing. "Get up there," he insisted.

"You don't have to be my submissive for the class if you don't want to." Master Cooney's quiet words drew my attention back to the dais. Light freckles spattered over his high cheekbones, his Grecian nose set over perfect lush lips with a Cupid's bow and teardrop. His jawline was shadowed by trimmed red scruff that appeared soft rather than abrasive.

He offered me a small smile, the kindness in his eyes a contradiction to the appearance of his massive bulk and looming presence.

I swallowed against sudden tears, realizing he reminded me of the teddy I'd held in bed as a child. Russet fur with the sweetest chocolate-brown eyes, Beary had offered comfort regardless of his small size. Master Cooney stood easily six feet over the size of my old stuffed animal, but the soothing effects of his attention calmed me all the same.

"I-I do want to," I whispered the truth I recognized in my trembling body.

"You have my permission as her Dom to touch her," Stephen stated, arrogance in his tone.

Master Cooney kept his focus on me and held out his hand. I realized I stared at his face and quickly lowered my gaze like a well-behaved sub ought to do. His wide palm and long fingers beckoned to me, offering me assistance onto the platform.

I slid my hand into his.

A shot of pure adrenaline rushed through my chest, doubling my heart rate in an instant. I inhaled a quick breath, my lungs filling with the spicy citrus cologne that had affected me in the lounge.

Divine. Delicious. Decadent.

All three words flitted through my brain, making my mouth water and my insides melt as I clung to his fingers and stepped up beside him. Regardless of my height, Master Cooney towered over me. Rather than feel intimidated and wishing to curl in on myself, I wanted to press in closer. Feel his warmth wrap around me. Protect me—

"Show Master Cooney what a sweet little sub you are, Becky," Stephen called out, his voice loud enough in the still room that I cringed.

"Have a seat," Master Cooney murmured, motioning to the chair sitting sideways on his right.

I perched on the seat's edge, facing my master for the next however long, my knees together and hands clasped in my lap. A glance over my shoulder revealed Stephen had found a vacant station near the middle of the group and sat on a chair, arms folded over his chest.

His stare promised punishment if I embarrassed him in any way.

Releasing a steady exhale, I lowered my gaze to the floor. My heartbeat refused to slow, and my stomach churned once more. Wishing the floor would open up and swallow me, I closed my eyes. Finding a state of calm would save me from sure humiliation—and angry fists once Stephen and I returned home.

But I was a bundle of nervous energy. Fear of the unknown and dreaded insecurities took me to an edge I didn't think I would find my way back from.

Chapter 5

Daniel

Needing to keep my focus on the task at hand rather than the alluring, timid woman sitting on my right, I went over some bondage safety basics about circulation problems and mobility issues. I pointed out the need to take care with pressure points to avoid nerve damage and encouraged constant communication between partners.

Since everyone in the room belonged to the club, I didn't bother with any BDSM basics—communication, safe-words, and consent.

Hopefully, my "winging it" proved informative and didn't sound stilted or boring to those just wanting to explore or learn a new kink.

Once finished with the preliminaries, I knelt on the floor in front of Becky, knowing I had my work cut out for me.

Waves of fear and unease reached through the space between us, but the same as when I'd seen her in the lounge, I got caught up in the woman's delicious curves. I wanted to tie knots against her flesh and string her up. Her smooth skin would bulge between the loops of my rope, her plump breasts and tightened nipples left free for my tongue and teeth.

Her nubs had grown hard.

Fucking hell.

Swallowing audibly, I attempted to talk my dick into staying flaccid for a change. Fuck knew an arrogant asshole like Stephen would be a raging jealous jerk if my tight leathers revealed what his woman did to me, regardless of how he'd insisted we scene together—that I had his permission to touch his property.

Thinking of the man studying us in my periphery calmed my heating blood and allowed me to glance over at Becky with a more thorough eye to get a read on her body language beyond the obvious unease hitching her shoulders toward her ears.

Faded bruises splotched over parts of her body that I hadn't noticed out in the dim lounge. A few still showed a darker purple, but most had faded to a dull yellow. I wondered about consent between her and Stephen. Red flags from his treatment of her earlier in the club's main area made me believe he took what he wanted, when he wanted. How the fuck he'd gotten admittance to Chantelle's, I had no fucking clue.

The club owner wouldn't have missed the obvious signs of abuse I couldn't dismiss considering what I'd seen and heard in the lounge.

Pushing aside all the questions ringing in my head, I focused on my task. I would make the demonstration good for Becky, the best I could considering who sat in the audience keeping watch over us.

"Do I have permission to touch you, Becky?" I asked for her ears alone, my tone low and soothing even though she made my heart race with yearning to fold her in my arms and keep her from harm.

She lifted her focus off the floor to glance over at her asshole partner again.

"This is *your* choice, Becky," I told her firmly, and she turned her wary eyes on me. "*You* hold the power on this stage—over my hands and my rope. Nothing happens that you don't agree to. Understand?"

Wetness welled over her brown irises even as her pupils swelled. "Yes, Sir," she whispered, voice inflecting surprise —and thankfulness.

The title she gifted me slid arousal slid through my blood, a worthy adversary to my self-control. "Do you have a safeword?" I asked, my voice still hushed.

Becky shook her head.

Fucking *shook. Her. Head.*

Heat rushed through me, a blinding light of rage I struggled to swallow down. The fucker leading her around on a leash didn't allow her a way to shut shit down? Who the fuck did he think he was? A real Dom would never allow a scene to take place without a way for the submissive to end things if they weren't comfortable.

Jesus Christ.

I bit my tongue, needing a minute to find my voice and trust myself to not go apeshit on the fucker I could feel studying my every move.

"If you want to stop," I stated, my tone nothing but husky, restrained passion for violence, "say stop. Everything ends. No questions asked. And if you feel any pain, odd twinges, tingling, or loss of sensation, you tell me that immediately too. Understand?"

"Yes, Sir," she whispered again.

My dick bucked, the anger coursing through me be damned.

"Can I have your hand?" I asked, my voice low and raspy, the fact she turned me on evident to anyone with ears and eyes.

She offered without hesitation, the trust in her eyes like a live wire linked directly to my groin. I'd never had an act of submission turn me on like that—and I gloried in it. Fucking loved the fact she believed in my intentions without hesitation.

There would be no hiding how Becky affected me.

Hopefully, the other dominants in the group would be just as aroused by what they did—and by their submissive partner's reactions to their touch.

Maybe Stephen wouldn't care. The man's presence alone screamed fragile masculinity, but the fact his woman made me hot might please him. Puff up his arrogance.

But fuck him and fuck his insecurity. I would make this good for his lovely submissive. For all those watching. And if Stephen caused shit, the bouncer at the exit could drag his ass from the room.

I slid my thumb across Becky's palm and up over her wrist. A shiver rippled over her body, her full lips parting on a quick inhale.

"Any pain or tingling," I asked as I gently probed around her hands and forearms, my dick still traveling up Swell-ville Boulevard.

"No, Sir."

Teeth gritted against a slew of emotions battling for my focus, I forced my attention on the petal softness of her wrists, forearms, and inner elbows, taking longer than I normally would have with another submissive...like Bunny. A woman who didn't turn me on.

Becky's shoulders relaxed beneath my gentle touch, and satisfaction filled my chest over bringing her pleasure while explaining to the class how to check pressure points and map out the area they wished to bind.

As though Becky's and my spirit intertwined through effortless glides of my fingertips over her skin, the tension easing from her coaxed mine to chill the fuck out as well.

When I knew I lingered too long in losing myself to having Becky under my hands, I tore myself away and picked up a bundle of hemp rope off the floor to address the class. "Go ahead and unravel one of the lengths that was on your chair."

While the small crowd did as told, I unwound one of mine, two ends tumbling from my hands to the floor as I angled to face the audience.

"The center of a folded rope is called bight, and that's a term I'll be using a lot. We'll start with the most basic, a single column tie."

I turned back to Becky to find her gaze latched on my face rather than the floor. Anticipation filled her warm eyes. Stephen wouldn't appreciate how she looked at me without permission, but my dick sure as fuck did.

"Hold out your right hand," I murmured to her.

She did as told, her upraised arm only slightly shaky. My balls ached at her simple act of obedience to my command.

"Take the bight and wrap it around your sub's arm just above the wrist, making sure to leave room for two fingers to pass between the rope and their skin," I told the class, brushing my fingertips over her softness again as I did another turn.

A slight whimper passed her lips, and I fought for calm.

Her knees pressed together, her ass shifting enough to

let me know my touch, my ropes binding her wrist, affected her in the same way it did me.

Unable to help myself, I glanced down between to the apex of her thick thighs and the dark, soft-looking curls hiding her pussy from sight. My chest rose on a deep inhale, but no sweet reward wafted past my nose.

I cleared my throat and addressed the group watching us. "Now, create a loop then pass the rope over and underneath. Once again through the loop—then tighten."

Becky lowered her head so her shoulder-length hair shielded her face from the audience as I continued with the same demonstration, tying her other wrist in the same way

Was it embarrassment that caused her to hide? Shame?

"Okay, Becky?" I murmured, wanting to tilt her chin up to better check in with her. I refrained but only because of the stare I could feel on the side of my face.

"Yes, Sir," Becky murmured.

I exhaled slowly, refocusing on my task, thankful my cock eased up in attempting to break free from my leathers and simply ached inside its prison. "The lead rope can then be attached to whatever you wish, even another part of the body." Moving to the side, I glanced over the group. "Subs, lift your arms so I can see the beauty your Doms have wrapped your wrists in." I paused, giving the group a quick perusal, noting Stephen peered at me with an arrogant smirk rather than heated rage over the fact I sported a raging boner. Thank *fuck*. "Well done, all of you. Moving on..."

The minutes passed too quickly.

I wanted to soak in the feel of Becky's skin while showing various bondage basics, intentionally brushing my fingertips over her more often than necessary. When I had her stand so I could demonstrate a chest harness, she moved with liquid grace when I'd expected stilted unease.

"You're doing so well, Becky," I whispered for her ears alone.

She shivered at the words of praise, making me wish I could rain down similar sentiments by the bucketload.

Taking care to avoid her heavy breasts, I circled her ribs several times, tying knots as needed.

Becky seemed to be in tune with my touch, taking cues from my light touches to turn her as I explained my work to those watching guests. She was a beautiful piece of art. Supple flesh. Hemp ropes. Submissive hunger.

"Are you all right, Becky?" I asked again to check in.

"Mmm," she murmured as though time had lost its meaning and she wanted nothing more than to float on air.

Fuck, did I want to give her that—to make her fly where nothing but peace and pleasure resided.

"Why don't the submissive partners sit down on their chairs," I said, a hand on Becky's shoulder, "and I'll walk you all through an example of sexual bondage."

Becky sank onto her seat, her legs parting slightly to offer me a glance between her thighs. Wetness smeared on her plump lower lips.

Lust rocketed through me, stringing my balls up tight to my groin.

No woman had ever instilled such an instant need inside me. Desperate desire to sink deep into her warmth and bring her to release warred with my control.

She isn't mine.

Her pussy was off-limits.

Stephen watched.

Slowing my inhales and focusing on those truths, I once more knelt before Becky, a length of rope in hand.

Her lips parted as she panted for breath.

I swallowed down a groan and the need to squeeze my

junk. "Will the fact you're turned on make your husband angry?" I couldn't help but whisper, my lips barely moving.

"He's not my husband," she was quick to point out, which made my heartbeat race, "but...maybe? I don't...I don't know."

My focus flitted to one of the faded bruises on her left cheekbone, thrilled as *fuck* to learn she wasn't as off-limits as I'd thought. "Should we end the demonstration?"

"No." The word flew from her lips, her gaze finally lifting to mine.

My breath left in a rush as a sense of...something strange, *dizzying*, passed between us. Potent didn't begin to describe the longing, the magnetic pull, to bury myself inside her. Make her mine.

"Please don't stop," she begged.

No fucking way I could deny her.

Lips pursed, I dipped my head and began the pressure point explanation to the audience, checking in with Becky as I searched for tingling or pain. Once I reached her ankle, I shifted her leg farther from the other, fighting like hell to keep from filling my vision with her bare folds.

"First, we're going to secure the ankle." Thank fuck I sounded professional and not like a man on the verge of rutting into a sopping pussy to empty his balls.

One ankle tied to the chair, I pulled the rope upward, looped it around the top of her calf, and secured it before using the rest of the rope to bind her wrist to the chair's arm.

Becky gently tested the rope as I stood, but no tension raised her shoulders, and no quick breaths of alarm lifted her gorgeous chest. She sank into her seat, in complete submission, a sweet smile curving her lips.

Fuck. My. Life.

Could she be any more perfect a submissive for my ropes?

Turning away when I wanted to stare, I inspected the audience's work, giving praise where earned.

A soft sigh sounded behind me, and I turned, lightly caressing Becky's knee because I couldn't *not* touch her in that moment of her relief. "Okay, sweetness?" I asked, the term of endearment smooth and as delicious on my tongue as honey.

"Yes, Sir.

Christ, this woman...

Chapter 6

Becky

Master Cooney pushed my left leg away from the other, sending a rush of cool air over my exposed core. My pulse thrummed in my ears, drowning out his voice as he spoke to his class about *sexual* binding. The warmth of his palm stroked down my calf. Hemp rope slid around my ankle, and he tied me to the chair. He took care to ease his fingers beneath the loops to make sure they weren't too tight and uncomfortable.

I didn't shy away from being made immobile but sank into the alluring calm teasing at the edge of reason.

Prickling tingles swept up my legs in the wake of his fingertips over my knee. My thighs. Tremors quaked inside me as he bound my flesh once more to the chair. He gripped the rope tied to my wrist and lashed that one the same as the right.

Spread open for him, I sat at his mercy, every inch of me relaxed. I'd never felt such freedom in my entire existence.

I drifted along the edge of something delicious. Alluring. A heady feeling floated through my body and thoughts.

Nothing mattered in that moment but Master Cooney and his assuring touch. The spicy citrus of his cologne filled my lungs, and his erotic ropes hugged my skin with addictive affection.

The audience mingled to my right, barely registering past the haze of desire hovering over me. Awareness that they would be unable to see the effects of Master Cooney between my thighs made falling into a semi-state of euphoria as easy as breathing.

His warm hand settled on my left knee, keeping me grounded when all I wanted to do was drift away. "You are so goddamn beautiful, Becky," he murmured, his voice haggard as though he'd never spoken truer words.

I wanted to laugh but couldn't. Simply staring like a simpleton, I yearned to be caught up in his piercing brown eyes and drown in the wetness he brought to life inside me.

He'd claimed I had the control. How wrong he'd been.

He leaned in slightly, the hunger in his gaze making goose bumps rise over my skin. "I wish we were alone so I could taste the nectar between your gorgeous thighs."

Oh, God. A shudder rippled through my core, a tingling awareness that spread upward to tighten my nipples into hard, aching points. At that moment, I realized what I experienced.

Master Cooney, his touch, his words, *aroused* me. He made my frigid body experience physical desire for the first time.

In front of an audience.

I swallowed hard as reality and awareness of Stephen's presence trickled into my conscience. My brain came back fully online as did self-consciousness and shame. Although I lusted for whatever would happen next, the scene between Master Cooney and I had to end. Immediately.

But would the gentle giant of a Dom listen to me? Had he meant what he'd said about my having the power to control the scene I'd consented to do with him? While unsure, considering how he'd put me under a spell of some sort, I had no choice but to try. Otherwise, that doom of humiliation I thought I'd face by agreeing to be his volunteer wouldn't compare to the anger Stephen would let me know about once we left the club.

I expected pain. Plenty of it. Angry words over how I had humiliated him by finding pleasure in a stranger instead of him. Guilt speared into my brain, making me want to curl up in on myself.

"S-Stop," I whispered.

Master Cooney's lustful gaze eased up the second the word stuttered from my lips.

"P-Please," I pleaded past the thickness growing in my throat. "Stephen c-can't see me—realize he wasn't the one to turn me on."

A soft, hissed curse passed between Master Cooney's thinned lips, but he didn't hesitate to pull out a sharp knife.

With quick precision, he freed me from my bonds that hadn't felt restrictive or threatening in any way. I'd enjoyed them, parts of my body rousing from a deep sleep with surprising force. Still, I quickly pressed my knees together once unbound, hiding the evidence of what had happened, how I'd responded to someone else's touch besides my long-time boyfriend.

Warmth flooded my chest and face, shame making me want to sink into the floor where I could hide. But the need in my core didn't relent. It remained, desperate to be heightened and coaxed to completion.

Master Cooney addressed the class, ending the demonstration and asking the Doms to release their submissive if they so wished.

I rubbed my wrists, fingers trailing over the slight indents left on my skin. They were beautiful, unlike the angry red marks from Stephen's rough-textured ropes. Trailing my fingertips over the pattern, I caught myself smiling, soaking in the memories I would cherish forever even though I felt guilty for wanting to do so. Maybe the class had been helpful for both of us, and Stephen had learned a better way to touch me, to use his ropes in a way I would enjoy.

Master Cooney squatted in front of me, but I kept my focus on the floor rather than facing the draw his eyes and body had on every cell inside me.

"Are you okay, Becky?"

I nodded, lying my ass off.

"Normally, I would take you in my arms and help bring you back down from where you hovered just now, but I think it's for the best if I don't."

"Thank you," I whispered, still unable to look at him.

"There's a bathroom just through that door," he said, keeping his voice low and gesturing toward the dais's end. "I'll make sure Stephen stays here while you take a few minutes to calm down, but if you need anything, please let me know, okay?"

I nodded, my voice taxed out.

He stood and stepped back, offering me his hand.

I wanted to touch him. Feel the steadying warmth of his fingertips ghosting over my skin.

But doing so outside of a scene wouldn't feel right—and I had abruptly ended ours with one simple word.

A sense of power slid through my blood as that truth

settled in my brain. *I had halted our scene—I had called the shots, and Master Cooney had listened.*

Following the enlightened thought came a rush of disappointment in how Stephen didn't allow me such a voice. I hoped he had paid attention and learned.

Murmurs of the other students filtered through my brain as I stood without Master Cooney's assistance and hurried on shaking legs toward the door he had indicated. Leaving him behind felt...*wrong* even though it was the right choice for me to make as Stephen's other half.

My damp thighs rubbed together with self-lubricated friction, refocusing my mind on my arousal. Fingers shaking, I pulled on the door handle, a sensor light flicking on overhead as I stepped over the threshold into a half bath. I clicked the lock shut behind me and breathed a sigh of relief at the silence, the lack of eyes following me.

So this is what it feels like to be turned on—and in charge.

An almost manic giggle escaped me, and I ran a fingertip through my slippery folds, trying to imagine how good Stephen's cock would feel thrusting with natural wetness easing his length's passage. I eased a finger up inside me, catching my breath. Need for more, to be filled completely, made a quiet moan echo in the stillness around me.

I'm not broken.

The truth slammed into my brain, and tears slid from my eyes as I removed my fingers from between my thighs. Smiling through my hazy eyesight, I wiped my pussy dry and washed my hands.

Perhaps now that my body had woken up, sex would no longer be a burden I would rather avoid. Perhaps Stephen would find joy in me rather than disappointment. Perhaps the love we'd had when we were younger *would* return, and I would once more have a voice in our relationship.

Clinging to hope, I headed toward the bathroom's exit, excitement in my heart and mind.

Chapter 7

Daniel

Stephen made his way toward the raised platform where I'd brought his woman's body to life. His gaze locked on me, a smirk I couldn't read on his lips.

I answered questions and offered suggestions for the attendees lingering around to come back the following Friday for Master Lamond's second class Chantelle had told me about. Too soon, the other members moved off, leaving me alone with Dom Wannabe.

At least my anger had dissolved into an annoying buzzing in my gut rather than a voracious hunger to break his face.

"My Becky was lovely tonight," Stephen said once I finally turned and gave him my full attention.

Of course, he used a possessive in front of her name.

"She was." I kept my tone neutral and reached for one of the coils of rope on the floor to keep my hands busy in an unharmful way. "She's a natural submissive. You're lucky to have her." Both statements were true, but I couldn't say the same about his ability as a Dom or her in landing the piece of shit she'd shown up with tonight.

They might not have been married, but it had been obvious by their interactions in the lounge and her concern for Stephen's insecurities over her being aroused by my ropes that they had been together for some time. Long enough that she remained off-limits no matter how badly I wanted to bind her up and send her soaring for real.

"No one else wanted her, so she was an easy catch." The sneer in Stephen's voice roused my anger.

"How long have you been together?" I forced myself to keep with the pleasantries rather than telling him to fuck off.

"Twelve years. We met our freshman year in high school."

"That's quite some time," I muttered, wrapping the rope and imagining it around Stephen's throat—tight enough he couldn't breathe.

"Yeah, we've been through a lot." He straightened his shoulders, thin lips twisting into a fake-ass smile. "She's a great slave, and the scenes I have of her on video..." He shook his head, gaze flitting to the bathroom door she had disappeared behind minutes earlier. "Becky holds nothing back. She's a vocal whore without the fake tears and laughable moans of real porn stars. We have over two thousand subscribers. You ought to check out my work sometime," he stated, as though 2k was something worth bragging over. He handed a card to me, and I told myself I only accepted it to get him to shut up and walk away before I beat his ass to a bloody pulp.

Fuck, I hated how he brought my violent side roaring to life.

"Ah, there's my Becky." A smile lifted his lips, but his expression held no love for the woman he called his.

Why the hell did he stay with her if—according to his

bitching earlier—she didn't get turned on when sceneing with him? Why bind a sub to your side if you didn't connect with them?

Scowling, I glanced at Becky as she walked toward us, hands clasped and head down, hair shielding her face. At least she'd maintained some of the relaxed stance keeping her from folding in on herself like it seemed she'd wanted to do before I'd tied her to the chair.

For her sake, I hoped she had erased all evidence of her arousal from between her thighs. If Stephen had been able to see the glistening on her thickened labia like I had, breathed in the honeyed scent of her, I felt sure he would have flown into a rage and tried to kick the shit out of me.

I barely held back a snort at the thought of him attempting to punch me let alone shove my mass.

"Enjoy yourself?" Stephen asked, clicking the leash back onto her collar.

"I suppose, Sir," she said with a trace of shakiness to her voice.

"Did Master Cooney's ropes get you all hot and bothered?" Stephen's tone hinted at threatening consequences if she said yes.

"Um...no?" she whispered as though picking up on what I had. Any good Dom would know she lied by the flinch and cower that tucked her body in on itself once more.

Not Stephen. He scowled as though disappointed by her answer when it had sounded like a negative was what he'd wanted to hear.

The asshole gave off vibes that caused serious brain whiplash.

"The fuck, Becky?" He turned and started stalking off, dragging her along behind him. "Not even getting tied up by a shibari master was enough to get your cunt juices flowing? There's seriously something wrong with you."

I saw red. Wanted to choke the life out of Stephen Wannabe Dom, Fuck-Face-Magee with my bare hands. Lusted to watch the light in his eyes dissipate until his soul fled to hell where it belonged. Motherfucker didn't realize—or just didn't give a shit—that his words hurt his woman worse than fists.

Becky followed along after him like a browbeaten dog, and I could only imagine the humiliation she must feel from the shit pouring from his lips.

The room cleared, and I threw the bundled ropes into the bin on the dais. I needed to stay and finish cleaning up, but couldn't. My feet turned toward the exit, and I hurried up the quiet hallway to the lounge.

Teeth gritted, I scanned the crowd, catching sight of Stephen and Becky. They weren't headed toward the locker rooms and exit as I'd expected.

I ordered a tonic and lime since there was no alcohol served at the bar and stood against a wall, acting the part of a bouncer like I oftentimes did when no one of interest caught my eye.

But someone definitely had—I just needed to keep back and watch over her from afar for as long as I could to make sure no shit went down with Stephen.

A minute later, Chantelle slipped into the lounge, something she hardly ever did, and skirted around the room toward me. She scanned the sexual smorgasbord and chatting members, calculating in her perusal as always.

She stood a few paces behind Becky for a while, her gaze resting on Stephen as he enjoyed an exhibitionist take a paddle to his submissive. While Stephen stroked himself through his cheap leather pants, Becky turned her head away from the scene.

I moved around the perimeter of the room, closing the distance between us. Stephen's eyes gleamed as he watched the Dom redden his sub's ass. He had that glint my dad always got right before he went on a beating spree.

Chantelle caught my attention with a small wave, instantly making me tug on the reins of my anger. She motioned me toward the reception area with an incline of her head.

I went where she'd suggested, but my gaze lingered on Becky until I was forced to turn and leave the lounge behind.

The double door leading into the entryway shut behind me, and I followed Chantelle into her office. "Have a seat," she said. While usually a master of hiding her feeling, her eyes blazed with the same emotion boiling my insides.

"Care to tell me what the hell is going on?" I scowled while settling onto the leather chair.

"Becky is my cousin—"

"Shit."

"—and I set up tonight because I wanted you to meet her."

I glowered, hating the thought that I'd been manipulated. Toyed with. Used for someone else's benefit. I'd had enough of that shit when I'd lived on Boston's streets when I'd first arrived. "Why?" I bit out the word.

"Because physically she's your kind of woman, the perfect submissive for you, and you're all too familiar with what she's living with right now."

The muscle in my jaw ticked even though her explanation was a hell of a lot better than I'd expected.

"I'm also sure she stays with Stephen out of insecurity.

Showing her she's beautiful and desired beyond him is the only thing that is going to set her free."

I forced my body to relax and exhaled slowly, trying to get hold of myself. "How bad is it?"

"Bad." Chantelle stared at me, still frowning. "Last I spoke with her a few months ago, she told me Stephen forbade her to see anyone outside of home and work. She also said that Stephen doesn't apologize or plead for forgiveness anymore when he hurts her."

"Fucking cocksucker." I swore a few more times, my hands fisting on my thighs. "Have you seen any of the videos Stephen brags about?"

"Yes, but I suggest you don't go looking for them."

I raised a brow.

"You'll go into a murderous rage and wind up in jail if you watch a single one."

"Fuck." I scrubbed a hand over my face, growling under my breath. She didn't know I'd experienced the first part of her prophecy once already.

"I need you to do next Friday's class."

"No fucking way." My tone left no room for argument.

"I'll pay you double for helping Becky." Chantelle pleading—never thought I'd see the day. And I knew why she'd tacked on her cousin's name. Doing so would bring her to my mind's eye. It would also tug on my protective nature for all persons and animals surviving abuse.

I hesitated, although I wanted to reiterate my previous answer. Fuck me, I really yearned to do what Chantelle said, but I told myself I wouldn't get involved. I had zero capacity for inserting myself between a couple that had been together for twelve years, especially when Becky turned me on the way she did.

Playing Chantelle's game would bring nothing but trouble.

And I wouldn't have my innocent age to keep me from that second part of her prophecy.

"You could easily send Stephen over the edge," Chantelle continued when I didn't reply, "make his true colors shine, and open Becky's eyes to the tyrant she's been living beneath since high school."

"And how the fuck am I supposed to do that when she is already uncomfortable in this environment?"

"She clearly enjoyed your ropes and touch."

"Security cameras keep you informed." I didn't bother asking. She'd been too confident in her statement and hadn't been in that room with us.

"Always," Chantelle said without a hint of remorse or shame in her voice. "You turned her on for the first time in her life—if what she's told me in the past is true."

I tipped my head back, eyes closed as my heart ached for the sweet woman who had come alive beneath my hands. "Goddamnit."

Clothing rustled, and I lowered my head to find Chantelle leaning forward, elbows on her desk. A glint lit her eyes and made me shift on the seat. "I'll bet wrapping her breasts in a chest harness and stringing her up would send her flying."

"You don't mean into subspace," I muttered, the images she created in my mind swelling my cock and loosening my fists.

The smirk on Chantelle's lips matched the mischief in her hazel eyes. "Stephen has never seen Becky climax—she never *has* climaxed. Another man fulfilling her in ways he hasn't been able to will set him off and give me a reason to have him removed from the premises. I'll finally have access to my cousin without his influence."

"And what happens when you kick his ass out of here?"

"Becky will stay with me, and before you ask, Stephen has no idea where I live."

I'd seen couples like them before, up close and fucking personal. Knew all too well how it worked when a woman didn't have an identity outside of her abuser. "And when she enters that excuse phase that will land her back in Stephen's grip?"

Her manicured nails tapped on her desk. "She's not going to make it to that point."

I frowned. Did she have some magic wand she hid on her body? "And why is that?"

Chantelle leaned toward me. "Because—" her voice lowered "—you're going to pursue Becky and quietly lay out Stephen if he comes sniffing around."

I huffed a snort of laughter even though I didn't find her plan amusing. "You're one calculating bitch."

She sat back, the Cheshire cat grin lifting her lips. "You have no idea."

"I'm not a violent man." I reminded her of what I wanted to remain true about my adulthood.

Chantelle stood and rounded her desk. "No, but I'm sure you could find a way to send him running, tail between his skinny-ass legs."

"Little man complex," I muttered, wanting to hear him squeal and cry how he made Becky.

"Like you wouldn't believe. Now—" she opened her office door and gestured me out "—rather than get your panties in a bunch from watching that asshole drag her around the lounge for the next hour or two, head home. Make a plan for next weekend."

Chapter 8

Becky

I had never known fear compared to the anxiety and tremors I experienced when we left Chantelle's. Thankfully, we hadn't run into Amber, and Stephen was none the wiser my cousin had titled her club after her middle name.

I sat in my long coat, still naked beneath, hands clasped on my lap and staring out the passenger window while Stephen drove. Inky black shrouded the sky until we arrived home forty-five minutes northwest of Boston and its nightlife.

We had driven in near silence, and my mind gnawed on what might be going through Stephen's head. Although somewhat sure he hadn't been aware of my body's response to Master Cooney, I couldn't help but chew on the inside of my lip. The coppery tang of blood tinged my saliva as I climbed from the car into the cold evening air, following Stephen up the stoop to the fixer-upper we had called home for five years. The place still resembled a ramshackle pile of old lumber, but we had a roof, heat, and electricity, so I didn't complain about the lack of progress he had made in fixing the house up like he'd planned to do.

Stephen unlocked the door and went in, leaving me to pass him by so he double-locked us in for the night as usual. He tossed the keys onto the small collect-all table I had placed in the entryway and strode toward the kitchen.

I started toward the stairs to change into my PJs.

"I want you naked and bent over the spanking bench when I come up, Becky!" he hollered as the treads squeaked beneath my feet.

Tears sprang to life, stinging my eyes.

Stephen had made me pleasure him with my mouth and hands while he had watched another sub get her ass beat in Chantelle's lounge, humiliating me beyond anything he'd ever done to me. Including the cross and ball gag video he had recorded and uploaded to that porn site. He bragged it was his best work, gaining the most views and comments, but I never watched or checked where he posted to. It was bad enough that I had to live through the events the first time.

Although numerous scenes had been acted out in Chantelle's lounge, I couldn't help but feel embarrassed taking him into my mouth and having him pull my hair while I worked and gagged to get him off.

He hadn't complained out loud like he usually did, but I felt his frustration and anger in the sting of my scalp and the thrust of his hips. Until he finally came in my mouth, my jaw had ached and my eyes watered.

We'd left not long afterward, my hopes for the two of us finding better footing once more fading.

I shrugged my coat off inside our bedroom, my gaze on the spanking bench he kept there rather than in the dungeon. The damn thing was homemade and had no padding. I often plucked splinters from my knees and chest after Stephen finished with me. I had asked for something to kneel on and rest against after the first use but ended up with cane welts for complaining that all his hard work in building the contraption wasn't good enough. He'd called me spoiled. Ungrateful.

Head hanging, I brought to mind the carefree, attentive young man I had known him as back in high school. It wasn't until a couple of years after graduation when life's responsibilities and work stress began to affect Stephen. He had grown unstable, an emotional roller coaster without an operator's control.

I agreed to his newest outlet he claimed he needed to calm himself, and although he didn't offer me aftercare in return for sceneing anymore, I wanted to think that he would heal.

My cousin was the only one who knew about Stephen's problems, and I had shared with her to get some advice on how to be a good submissive. She had called Stephen's treatment of me abuse, but I remembered the old Stephen and knew that caring part of him just lay dormant inside.

Footsteps squeaked on the stairs beyond our opened bedroom door, and I quickly climbed onto the bench, clenching my eyes shut.

"You were a good sub tonight, Becky."

His words warmed me, easing my anxiety enough that I slumped on the wooden contraption I despised. I listened as he pulled off the pants he'd bought with the money we'd been saving for a new range since two burners on the current one in our kitchen didn't work.

"I think I'm in the mood for the flogger tonight."

Relieved he hadn't chosen his favored cane, I exhaled a sigh. "Thank you, Sir."

A whoosh of air, and I jolted forward at the impact, shrieking as he enjoyed. The quicker he got turned on again, the sooner he would take me from behind and be done for the night. At least the toy he'd chosen didn't hurt as badly as the cane.

I prayed for the arousal I'd felt at Master Cooney's touch, but my body didn't respond to Stephen. Whatever tingling the shibari master had induced between my thighs refused to rise up and ease my suffering as lash after lash rained across my back and thighs. Even slight pain held no pleasure for me, nor would it ever. God knew Stephen had tried to convince me otherwise one too many times.

But ropes? What if he caressed me as Master Cooney had while binding my wrists? What if Stephen took care in checking to make sure my circulation didn't cut off? What if he promised to give me control over the scene, to end it if I didn't feel comfortable?

The words of praise Master Cooney had poured down over me whispered through my head. I remembered his scent. How his eyes had hungered for me.

My breasts went heavy, and an ache settled in my nipples regardless of the stinging swats Stephen laid on me. Master Cooney had wanted to feast between my thighs—called my arousal nectar.

Oh, God.

I gulped, letting out another whimper. I couldn't think of him, couldn't allow myself to be aroused by someone else. I couldn't do that to the man I'd loved for twelve years. Couldn't stand the idea of disloyalty even emotionally.

The shame shattered through my body's attempt to rouse pleasure. I focused on the stinging strips of leather lashing against my lower thighs, too damn near to the backs of my knees for comfort. Stephen knew my sensitivity there and yet he continued downward, ripping shrieks from my lips once more.

I sobbed. Begged him to stop.

He didn't, but at least he didn't belittle or holler at me over whatever had set him off. Maybe he just needed to vent pent-up aggression that my two blow jobs hadn't fully satisfied since dinner. Perhaps Chantelle's had been overwhelming, had gotten him too worked up.

If that was the case, I had no wish to ever return—I would find some excuse to get out of going to the second class on the following Friday as he'd informed me we would be doing.

I lost count of the strikes and drained my tear reserves long before Stephen finally shoved into me with nothing more than his pre-cum to ease the way. Somehow, I managed to keep my lips clamped shut even though his fucking into me stung like a bitch.

Three pumps and he finished.

Sagging against the bench, I waited to see what he would do.

He turned on the shower and came back for me, helping me up.

Sobs wanted to rip from my throat, but knowing an emotional upheaval would only set him off again, I leaned into his sweating body and allowed him to lead me into the bathroom.

"You did well tonight," he said and kissed me on the forehead.

I blinked, hope attempting to rise inside my chest. When he handed me a cloth, I gladly washed him clean beneath the spray. And when he turned to do the same for me? I was thankful for the water pouring down between us that hid my tears of relief.

Chapter 9

Daniel

Somehow, I made it through Friday night and Saturday afternoon without utilizing that card Stephen had given me.

But not knowing what he'd done in those videos ate at my insides.

Thank fuck I had a booking with Elite on Saturday night. They didn't expect dick, so I didn't bother with a blue pill. Nothing about the customer wishing to experience bondage for the first time turned me on. I tied her as I'd done with Becky without even planning to. Like the sweetest sub I'd ever met, the client became aroused.

I enjoyed every second seeing Becky in my mind's eye. Checked in dozens of times with the client. Explained what I did and why...and how all Doms ought to do the same. Once I finished, she left a wet puddle on the chair, and it had only taken a single swipe of my thumb over her clit that she begged for to set her off.

We snuggled for over an hour, and I listened as she spilled the baggage of her life. As though my ropes had made me a therapist or counselor in her eyes, she opened her floodgates. I wanted to be moved by the fact her ex had an affair. That he'd stripped her rights to their home in Tuscany and the yacht he'd named after her.

At least they didn't have kids together, so there was that.

The woman couldn't have been more than thirty, still had a rocking body and enough money from the divorce settlement to draw in a crowd of men to choose from once she allowed herself to look for love again.

Rather than become invested as I did with most clients, I couldn't keep my mind off Becky. What had happened when she and Stephen had gotten home. How he'd treated her. If he'd kept his hands to himself.

I imagined that he had so as not to upset myself.

Sunday was my turn to host my friends for the Bruins game and helped to keep me distracted. Jarod canceled, big surprise, and Micah showed up first, a six-pack of IPA and chips and guacamole in hand.

"How was the new client last night?" he asked while setting his snack contributions on the coffee table in front of one of my two couches.

"Pliant, sweet, and definitely into bondage." I expected she would become a regular.

"She get your blood going?"

I accepted one of the beers he offered and led the way into the living room. "Nope."

Micah was aware of my issues—whatever they were. I had no fucking clue how to label myself and didn't really care if I ever figured my sexual shit out. "Can't say I'm sorry," he stated with a chuckle.

"Fucker," I muttered without heat, knowing he teased and just didn't want to lose me as an employee. As the only shibari master, I made him a pretty penny every month. Myself too. I didn't need to keep the day job in communications but didn't plan on being an Elite for life. Besides, the 401k kicked ass, and the extra income from EE allowed me to stockpile savings for whatever future endeavor floated my boat.

Maybe my own yacht.

A home in Tuscany.

But that would be years down the road if ever, and I doubted I would thoroughly enjoy either without having someone to share them with.

Becky.

Teeth gritted, I focused on Micah telling me about his little brother Sean being all up his ass to open a gay branch of Elite. I'd heard the argument between the two a couple of times over the previous months. Micah claimed Grindr was easy as fuck to utilize. Why would gay or bi dudes pay big bucks for what was easily attained? Sean shot back that straight hookup apps existed too and yet Elite still made Micah a rich man.

I expected the poking to continue, and my thoughts proved right. Within minutes of Sean showing up with his best friend Drake, the two brothers went at it. As far as I was aware, it was the first time Drake had heard the argument.

He sat silent, watchful—same as me. We sipped our beers while waiting for the Bruins to take to the ice as Sean hounded Micah. Twelve years older, Micah tended to treat Sean like the younger pup he was: untamed and half-wild. The guy was in his late twenties but still acted like a frat boy with his heart set on partying until he became too old and feeble to do so. Sean was also highly sexual and couldn't get enough dick.

He was passionate as hell about starting up what he

called EEMM. Elite Escorts Male on Male. Had his damn heart set on it.

"Tell him, Drake," Sean said, pink flushing his cheeks, his blue eyes flashing with excitement and hints of annoyance due to his brother denying him. "Tell this pussy-hungry asshole that a gay branch would be just as lucrative. Tell him about all the gay guys we know who are so damn deep in the closet they'd pay thousands for hookups if it meant keeping their images *clean*." He sneered the last word as though having been personally offended by a man's desire to do that very thing.

"I've never been closeted," Drake said with a shrug, "but those guys definitely exist. And the ones with pocket change to spare would certainly pay for safer options and hookups. Sean said you do NDAs for both clients and employees?"

Micah nodded, his lips in a thin line while studying Sean's best friend.

Compared to Sean, Drake was a big brute almost as tall as me, cut as fuck with dark hair and serious blue eyes. I wasn't above recognizing the guy was good-looking, but dick didn't do shit for me, same as most pussies.

"I'm going to have to agree with Sean then," Drake said and sipped his beer. "Gay men would do the same as your straight clients who wish to hook up without the hassle of trying too hard and who want the option to hide their activities."

"*Hard*," Sean whispered like the immature idiot he was.

Micah didn't respond and turned his focus back on the woman singing the National Anthem.

Sean belted out the lyrics at the top of his lungs in perfect tune. The kid had no filter in any way, shape, or form. He made me smirk more often than not.

"I have a couple more friends along with Drake who would love to be on your payroll," Sean started back in the second the song ended.

Micah glanced over at Drake. "You're interested?"

Drake shrugged. "I'd think about it, sure. Not like I'm looking for a relationship anytime soon."

"What about you, Cooney?" Micah asked.

"I don't do dick," I stated firmly, having had my fill of that when I'd done what I had to do to survive my first couple of months in Boston.

"No—I meant do you know of any gay men in the kink world who might consider signing on with Elite?"

Sean got really antsy, really quickly, shifting around with excitement lighting him up from the inside out. The kid was pure sunshine in fleshly form.

I thought about the other Doms who frequented Chantelle's but wasn't sure if any of them swayed the dick way. "Master Lamond is straight," I finally offered, "but he doesn't discriminate against tying up one sex over the other. I've seen him jack a sub off over at Chantelle's, but that doesn't mean he'll give or take dick up the ass."

Micah nodded, probably knowing the guy I spoke of. Micah had been a patron of Chantelle's longer than I had. He was the one who'd introduced me to the club owner and had gotten me the invite to join.

"Seeeee!" Sean dragged the word out, making Micah roll his eyes. "You have to do this for me!"

"You're a spoiled, fucking brat," Micah grumbled at his brother while pushing up to his feet. "You just don't want to have to work for dick—why should I expand my business to pay for your favorite hobby?"

"Because you love me," Sean sang the words, laughing. "Grab me and Drake another beer, would ya?"

Still muttering under his breath, Micah turned into the kitchen.

I chuckled, listening to Sean babble on to Drake about how his brother would hook them up with all the free dick and balls a gay man could wish for.

At least the banter kept my focus off Becky and the ache between my legs.

JE

I stared at Stephen's damn card for over an hour while trying to get my head straight. To watch or not to watch those videos Chantelle had warned me about? How badly did I want to lose my shit? Would I even last until Friday night before seeking the fucker out to rip his throat out if my concerns proved right?

The not knowing ate at my thoughts once the guys left Sunday night, and I couldn't let it go.

Tossing the card onto my coffee table, I scowled and headed into my home office. I'd memorized the porn site's address and typed in the search bar the name Stephen used to upload. My index finger didn't hover. I hit enter without hesitation, steeling myself for another rage flare up.

Still preview images lined the screen, and my jaw ticked from a brief glance.

Becky on a spanking bench.

Becky tied spread eagle to a bed.

Becky bent over the back of a couch, red handprints over her bare backside.

Growling, I jerked my focus to the top image and clicked on it.

Cuffed to a cross and ball-gagged, Becky blubbered and shook, cane welts covering her stomach and thighs. She wasn't trembling from the need to come, and it sure as hell wasn't subspace that hung her head.

My stomach churned with burning bile wanting to spew up my throat. Pitiful whimpers escaped her lips, a sob hitching her chest and making her heavy breasts jiggle.

Stephen walked around her with a handheld camera. "You're such a precious *little* sub," he crooned, sarcastic emphasis on little as though making fun of her plus-sized beauty.

Fucking bastard.

The lush woman deserved to be loved on by someone who thoroughly enjoyed all her curves. Flesh to grope and hold onto while burrowing deep inside her core.

"Fuck."

I closed the browser window without watching another second and stalked back out to my mini-bar, sickened and aroused at the same time. I'd had a couple of beers with the guys, but a double Grey Goose in one shot burned fire to my gut.

I still saw red. Wanted to sink into Becky's slick heat and lose myself in the woman who had wholeheartedly captured my attention.

The memory of the trust in Becky's eyes slammed me in the chest, and I rubbed a hand over my pecs, groaning. No fucking way I could ignore her unexpected presence in my life. No fucking way I could set the memory of her from my mind. And no fucking *way* would I allow a man to hurt yet another woman I'd come to care about even if I'd only known her a mere forty-eight hours.

"Fuck not getting involved. I'm going to free you whether you want it or not," I vowed to my living room as though Becky could hear me. "And God help Stephen if he attempts to stop me."

Chapter 10

Becky

Stephen took it easy on me all week, and by the time Friday rolled around again, our second and last night at Chantelle's, I held hope that another experience at the club would settle Stephen fully back into the man I'd seen glimpses of throughout the week.

He hadn't hurled insults at me over my inability to perform for him while sceneing and videotaping us, nor had he complained about my lack of arousal.

As with our visit the week before, my cousin was nowhere to be seen when we arrived. The same young woman who'd welcomed us the first time showed me into the lady's changing room. I exited into the lounge by myself, finding Stephen waiting for me just beyond the door as he had the Friday before.

I handed the key to the locker I'd placed my coat in to Stephen. He didn't spare me a second glance while shoving it into his leather pants pocket. His eyes lit with excitement, and pink stained his cheeks. Clasping my lead rope, he led me deeper into the lounge.

Gaze once more on the floor, I followed where Stephen

went. I kept my eyes downcast, refusing to give in to the temptation to look around for Master Cooney. I had dreamed about him on Wednesday night—his gentle touch, kind eyes, and deep rumbly voice.

I'd woken up damp between my thighs and aching to be filled, but I'd escaped our bed and calmed myself down rather than allowing Stephen the opportunity to ask why I suddenly felt the need to initiate intimacy, which I'd longed to do. He would never believe a single excuse I offered for the state of my desire.

Pushing aside thoughts of my miserable sex life, I thought about the shibari master.

Would he be teaching the class again? Would Stephen push me forward to volunteer? I feared being turned on again by Master Cooney—I had no doubt it would happen the second I smelled his citrusy cologne or felt his presence nearby. I feared Stephen's reaction if he found out how the man affected me. Such an event wouldn't further Stephen's growth.

I also didn't want to be on display, either. Not that I would have much choice if Stephen offered me as tribute. Master Cooney might ask for my consent, but denying him would only piss Stephen off.

Chewing the inside of my lip, I fought to keep from wringing my hands.

Stephen stopped for a time beside a sub on her knees pleasing her Sir, something he was quite fond of being on the receiving end of.

"See how deep she takes him?" Stephen said, tugging me forward. "She hollows her cheeks and sucks his cock with no gagging or tears."

I glanced up at the dark-haired woman beautiful enough to be a model. She gazed up at her Viking-like Dom, lust and love shining on her expressive face as she worked him over. Her Sir stared at her with the same emotion in his blue eyes as she had in hers.

"That's it, Bella," he murmured, winding his fingers gently in her hair, allowing his sub to control the scene. "Just like that…"

I glanced away, my throat tight. I'd never once been looked at with such adoration.

But, Stephen loved me. He proclaimed it with tears every time he apologized for hurting me. Or he used to, anyway.

I swallowed against the thickness wanting to close off my breaths, silent as he led me farther into the lounge. Swats sounded, followed by groans, and we stopped again.

Stephen made himself comfortable on a chair and pointed at the floor.

I lowered and tucked my knees beneath my belly, placing my forearms on the floor so he could prop his feet upon my back like he did sometimes at home while watching porn. My large breasts squashed beneath me, one angling out to the side beneath my chest, but I knew better than to tuck it back beneath me.

In my periphery, a sub lay over her Sir's lap, jolting and moaning with each smack to her ass and thighs.

Bent over in the stool position, I knew my backside was on full display with its dimples and cellulite. I closed my eyes and tried to go to that happy place Master Cooney had taken me to.

A quiet mind. Peace like I'd never experienced.

Minutes passed, and the woman's moans and her Sir's murmurings of what a good little sub she was fell on my ears. By the time they finished and Stephen pulled me to my feet, my knees and back ached, and jealousy swarmed deep in my heart.

I could handle Stephen's kink if he used words of affection and softer touches on occasion. I would gladly humble myself and submit without hesitation if he lavished love on me as that Viking god had with his Bella.

A ding rang twice atop the soft music from overhead, announcing the shibari class was about to start.

Butterflies erupted in my stomach as I shuffled along behind Stephen, quickly taking my mind from despondency.

Cooler than the lounge, the smaller room where we'd had the presentation the weekend before made my skin pebble. Purely from the temperature, I told myself. It had nothing to do with the citrus scent in the air or the bass voice welcoming us in and inviting us to claim a station for the class.

Stephen sat near the back, and I kneeled beside his chair where he pointed to. I peeked up through my lashes.

Master Cooney filled out his black leathers ten times better than Stephen could ever dream of doing. Thick, muscular thighs, a bulge my mouth began drooling to taste. Rippled abdominal muscles led upward to prominent pectorals, which spread outward into wide shoulders. He was a mountain of a man, every inch of him a magnetic tuning fork to my gaze and body.

The dimpled chin covered in clipped red whiskers, his square jaw, and Grecian nose. Dark eyes staring into mine...

Wetness rushed to my vaginal walls, and I felt instantaneous need. To be touched. To be filled.

Face hot, I lowered my head. I shouldn't have such wants, such desires for someone other than Stephen. My pulse thrummed in my ears, and my hands trembled where they lay palm up on my thighs.

"Stephen," Master Cooney called out once the class quieted. "Would you be willing to offer Becky's assistance again this evening?"

My breath caught.

No, no, no...

I bit my lip as Stephen stood and tugged on my lead rope.

"Of course. My Becky would love nothing more."

Face flaming and legs trembling, I followed him toward the platform where he unclasped my rope and told me to climb up and assist Master Cooney in showing the class how to be a proper submissive.

Shame flooded through me, but I accepted Master Cooney's outstretched hand. Electrical currents rushed up my arm and settled in my nipples at his warm clasp around my fingers. He released his hold too soon—not soon enough.

No chair sat awaiting me, so I stood shivering, covering the apex of my thighs with shaking hands, my focus on the floor where it belonged.

"Tonight," Master Cooney began in his low voice, "I'll be showing some more complex knots. I've made handouts, which you should have found on your chairs."

Papers rustled, and Master Cooney retrieved a coiled, red rope in my periphery. "Tonight, I'll be using hemp as I'll be suspending my lovely assistant."

I bit back my snort of laughter. Suspend me? I glanced up at the rope overhead attached to a ring fixed in the ceiling. Did he not see the size of my ass and thighs?

He stood before me, his back to the rest of the room. "Becky, look at me."

I lifted my head without hesitation, and an all-consuming desire for him rushed through me once more at the hunger in his warm eyes.

"May I touch you?" he murmured, his asking permission making my core clench.

I managed to nod.

He smiled as though thoroughly pleased by my consent, the same kindness I'd seen the weekend before in his steady gaze easing my discomfort at being the center of attention. "Your hair looks lovely tonight," he whispered.

Tears stung my eyes. I had spent a half hour curling my hair in loose loops to caress over my collarbones like Stephen loved. My boyfriend hadn't mentioned them, but at least he hadn't given me grief over taking too long to ready myself for the night.

Master Cooney's gaze dropped to my lips, and mine parted as I quickly inhaled. His smile dissolved, and hunger filled his eyes. His stare sent blood pulsing through my center, and a low moan escaped me.

His brow rose along with a corner of his mouth. "Are you ready, sweetness?"

The same pet name as the weekend before. Wetness hazed my vision as I nodded.

"You remember your safeword?"

"Stop, Sir," I whispered.

"And if I asked you for a color?" he questioned, still studying my face as though gauging my reaction.

I swallowed, knowing he spoke of the stoplight system I'd read about while on break from work the day before. I'd realized that everything Stephen and I did together in the lifestyle wasn't correct. But, I hadn't brought it to his attention—hadn't wanted to stir up shit when things had seemed decent for almost a week straight.

"Green, Sir," I finally whispered, my heart heavy.

Satisfaction emanated from Master Cooney's stare, and I swore the man was readying to rain praises down over me. "I'm going to wrap you in a chest harness first," he said instead of what I could have used in that moment to boost my spirits.

"O-okay."

"You remember that you're in charge, right? That you simply need to say stop or red to end things if you grow uncomfortable?"

"Yes, Sir."

"I really hope you don't this time, Becky, but I will not be angry with you if you do."

Unable to find my voice, I nodded, trusting his word.

Master Cooney turned me sideways with a light touch to my hip, putting me into profile for the audience. "Let's begin," he told the class.

Peace swept in with the brush of the hemp rope over my breast. His low voice rumbled in my ears, and as with the first time he tied me in his ropes, I moved with his slightest lead, the gentlest pressure to aid in his harnessing me.

The rope grazed over the hardened peaks of my heavy breasts, and I bit the inside of my lip, holding in my groan. His thumb brushed over my nipple, but rather than flinching or opening my eyes, I leaned into his touch. He wrapped my breasts tightly without pain, my contracted nipples squeezed between the rope.

The juncture between my thighs throbbed. Warm wetness seeped from me, coating my thighs. My ears rang. Every nerve ending in my body needed yet resisted that happy place that called from the back of my mind.

I lost who I was. Where we were no longer mattered. Master Cooney held my body's full focus.

He laid me on a mat on the floor, his hands and rope wrapping one of my legs, knotting me tight.

"So beautiful," he murmured, his fingertips fluttering along my thigh as he tied another loop. "So soft."

I melted, a smile on my face.

His fingertip brushed through the wetness near my swollen folds, and I lifted toward him, so, so needy...

"You're wet," he whispered, which made my eyelids flutter open. He stared between my thighs and continued tying. A few more instructions in his bass voice to the onlookers I didn't care about, and he turned his focus to my face.

Oh, sweet Lord...

I had never been on the receiving end of such a lustful look. His thumb rubbed along the inside of my thigh, hidden from sight from those on the floor to my right. "Are you ready to fly, sweetness?"

"Yes," I whispered on the edge of some unnamable cliff, every cell inside me buzzing and yet relaxed at the same time.

Master Cooney stood, connected the rope dangling from the ceiling to my harness, and I closed my eyes.

Without a grunt of effort, he hoisted me into the air. Hanging only by the connection points in knots on my thighs and chest harness, I swung up off the floor, the loops around my chest tightening on my breasts, pinching my nipples.

I moaned while floating, the intense longing in my core consuming me.

Sir's hand slid over my calf, rubbing my skin plumped between his ropes, creeping up my thigh...higher...

He spun me a half turn, his thumb rubbing over my pubic hair, gently flicking my throbbing clit.

A gale of exquisite torture slid upward from my toes, and I shuddered, whimpering.

He flicked again.

My nerve endings shattered, and I cried out as my first-ever climax swept me into bursting lights and pulsing, blinding pleasure. Warmth and wetness rushed through me, every contraction in my core pulling noises of euphoria from my lungs.

Cocooned in Sir's ropes—his hold—my tingling body floated into peaceful nothing.

Chapter 11

Daniel

Becky's cries of release echoed in my ears. I'd never heard—or seen—anything so goddamned beautiful in my life.

"The fuck?" Stephen cursed, his hiss radiating through the suddenly quiet classroom.

From the corner of my eye, I made note of him rising to his feet, and the two bouncers Chantelle had standing just inside the door tensed, but I couldn't tear my gaze from Becky as she swung in front of me, free and floating in subspace.

"The fuck?" Stephen's voice raised, and I finally turned toward him, uncaring of my raging hard-on. Murder lit his gaze, his open guppy mouth sputtering and spitting, but no sound came out. He lunged forward, but the bouncers reacted faster than his skinny ass could move. They grabbed hold of both his arms.

"Get the fuck off me!" He thrashed, but the bouncers dragged him away.

The door closed and shut out his heightening rant.

Fully soundproofed, the room didn't allow a single muffled holler to reach my ears.

I glanced at Becky.

She still hung suspended, relaxed and quiet, her dark curls hanging toward the dais beneath her.

"I apologize for the interruption," I stated quietly, turning toward the other couples on the floor in front of me, wanting them gone. Most subs sat in various stages of the harnessing I'd tied onto Becky. "I believe that does it for the evening. Thank you for attending."

Murmurs broke out as I returned my attention to Becky, soothing my hands over her one straight leg, up along her soft stomach, and over to her other leg I had bound ankle to thigh with a frog tie. Wetness coated her thick pussy lips and dripped into her ass crack.

My mouth watered.

Two steps brought me to her torso, and I gazed at her bound breasts, the crisscrossing ropes squeezing both plump nipples. Her head hung back, silken hair falling away from her peaceful face.

A half-smile curved her lips, and pink stained her cheeks.

Becky will be mine, I vowed to myself. *Mine to defend. Mine to worship. Soon.*

I ran the back of my hand down her neck, and she shuddered a sigh. "I'm going to lower you now," I whispered.

Taking my time, I untied the rope holding her suspended her in the air and gently lowered her to the mat. She rested as though sleeping and didn't move as I unknotted and unbound her legs.

The room slowly emptied, and once Becky lay naked, my rope indents marring her petal-soft skin, we were alone as I'd wished for.

I sat on the floor beside her and gathered her onto my lap, smoothing her hair from her forehead. My cock throbbed inside of my leather pants, pressing against her lush backside for long, agonizing minutes. I wanted nothing more than to slide between her thick-as-honey thighs and sink deep into her until her cream coated my drawn-up balls.

"You were so beautiful, sweetness," I murmured while trailing my knuckles over the tops of her breasts. Her nipples contracted, and she finally started to rouse, shifting in my arms with a sigh. "Becky?"

"Hmm?" Her eyelids fluttered open, and I drowned in her sated, trusting gaze. Like the strongest coffee, her dark-chocolate eyes were framed by long, black lashes.

"Welcome back." I smiled and continued running my hand over her body, the swells and dips of pure perfection, careful to avoid erogenous zones.

The corners of her lips rose again.

"How do you feel?"

"Amazing," she murmured, turning her face into my chest. "You smell so good."

I chuckled and squeezed her tight with one arm while resting the other on her hip.

We sat in silence for a few moments as I gave her time to come down. I knew the moment reality settled back over her brain—she stiffened in my arms.

"Shh..." I kissed her forehead.

"Where's Stephen?"

"In Chantelle's office, most likely."

Some of the tension left her limbs. "I...climaxed."

"You did," I said, my lips returning to graze over her forehead.

"Oh, my God." She clenched her eyes shut and

frowned, her face flushing red. "That's the first time... Stephen..."

"He wasn't happy."

Becky pulled from my hold, and although I yearned to keep her close, I let her go. She sat, knees drawn up and face buried in her arms. A shudder rippled through her, and I wrapped an arm around her shoulder, drawing her trembling form against me.

"He's going to hurt me," she whispered. "You too."

"He's not going to touch either of us." I rubbed one hand along her back while reaching for a bottle of water I'd left nearby. "Here." I uncapped and handed it to her.

She lifted her head and glanced around the room before taking my offer. Her smooth throat worked while sucking down the water.

The fear in her eyes remained after she finished, palpable and twisting my stomach.

I clenched my jaw against the need to break Stephen. "How about you go to the bathroom and clean up, then we'll go talk to Chantelle?"

She nodded, and I helped her stand, thankful as fuck she'd taken my offered hand and managed to move seemingly well for how hard she'd climaxed and soared for me.

Her ass jiggled as she shuffled away, and I groaned. Her scent still clung to my nostrils. I lifted my hand I'd brushed over her clit to my nose and inhaled deeply, filling my lungs. Sweet and musky—God, how I wanted to explore her folds with my tongue, lips, and teeth.

Not until Stephen was a part of her past and she was ready to move on though. I refused to further any guilt she might feel for climaxing for me and not her asshole boyfriend.

I satisfied myself by licking over my fingers, catching a

hint of her sweetness. My mouth watered for more.

Fighting off a raging boner, I wrapped up the ropes I'd used on her with precise slowness and determined focus.

Once Becky returned from the bathroom, face still pink and eyes wary, I took her hand without asking, still in a half-state of hardness. She didn't tug away but moved in close as though needing comfort or hoping she could draw from my strength.

We walked the carpeted hallway in silence while I attempted to keep rising tension from owning my muscles. The rest of the evening belonged to Chantelle and whatever plan she had set up in that devious mind of hers.

We entered the lounge, and Becky tugged her hand from mine, stepping behind me, head down and shoulders slumped. Anger flared, and I pulled her back up alongside me, wrapping my hand around hers. "We're not sceneing and you're not my sub." *Yet*, I wanted to add. "I want you to walk with me."

She lifted her gaze to my face, eyes widened and inquisitive.

Offering a reassuring smile, I headed toward the lounge's double doors leading to the entryway.

Chantelle had told me she would have Stephen wrangled into her office if he reacted to Becky's release like she'd expected him to. She had said she would hold him there until Becky was calm and ready for the confrontation.

"Go get dressed," I said, nodding toward the women's locker room off the reception area.

"I only have a coat," Becky said, "and Stephen has the key to the locker in his front pocket."

Fucking dead of winter, and that asshole didn't allow her any clothing. Talk about a complete hard-on killer. "There are robes on the back of the stall doors," I told her, barely suppressing the anger from leaking into my voice. "Grab one of those for now."

She returned a minute later, a navy-blue silk robe covering her from breasts to mid-thigh.

"Ready?" I asked, telling myself to focus on the task at hand rather than fantasizing about stripping her down again.

Face pale and lower lip between her teeth, she shook her head.

"I'll be right there beside you, and there are two bouncers with Stephen. I promise he won't touch you."

"O-okay."

I offered her a smile of reassurance before knocking on the door. One of the bouncers answered and stepped once more into position beside the office entrance, legs spread and arms crossed.

"Come in," Chantelle called from inside.

"Ladies first." I laid my hand on Becky's lower back, and she trembled beneath my touch. She stepped over the threshold, and I followed on her heels like a protective papa bear.

"You lying, conniving bitch," Stephen spat, standing from the couch to our left.

Titus, the bouncer standing beside him, grasped Stephen's shoulder and forced him down with an effortless shove.

"Cock-sucking whore," Stephen continued to spew while glowering. "You'll give in to the jolly green fucking red-headed giant and hold back your orgasms from me for twelve fucking years? You're nothing—"

"Enough." Chantelle's Domme voice cut Stephen clean off, his trap slamming shut.

Ball-less pussy. I wanted to laugh. He was all fucking talk.

Chantelle rounded her desk and hugged Becky. Indiscernible whispers passed between the two women before Chantelle led her cousin to the chair facing her desk. "Care to tell me what happened?" she asked, perching on the edge of her desk between Becky and Stephen.

Becky glanced over her shoulder at me, a flush rising up her face. "I ... uh..." She cleared her throat and turned back around. "Stephen volunteered me to be Master Cooney's assistant," she whispered, lowering her gaze.

"Go on," Chantelle said as Stephen muttered something under his breath.

"He tied me up."

"And?" Chantelle prompted even though Becky's tone and slumped shoulders said she didn't wish to continue.

I didn't care for the way she put Becky on the spot, making her uncomfortable in front of me and two other men, but she'd asked me to trust her, so I bit my tongue.

Becky glanced toward Stephen.

"Whore." He spat on Chantelle's carpet.

Becky jerked her face forward once more, cowering.

I clenched my fist as Chantelle ignored Stephen's outburst. "What happened, Becky?"

"I-I..."

"She had her first fucking orgasm," Stephen answered for her with a scowl, his eyes hard. "Unfaithful bitch supposedly can't come with me for all the years I've taken care of her, and she gets off without anyone touching her dry cunt."

Chantelle turned toward Stephen as Becky curled inward even more.

"I hardly think her cunt was dry if she orgasmed.

Perhaps the problem is *yours*, sir," she mocked him with a title he didn't deserve any more than he did Becky's loyalty for so damn long.

But I knew what went down in abused women's heads. I'd seen it. Had heard it.

"It's not my motherfucking problem!" Steam should have rolled from Stephen's ears at his raised voice. "Not *my* fucking problem!" he hollered again. "I've put in every effort to help her orgasm! Every kink imaginable, and she never allowed herself to respond to me. Never! Canes. Whips. Chains. I've fucked her every which way, every hole, and she's always refused me!"

"Is it true that you don't willingly give Stephen your climax?" Chantelle asked Becky, her voice soft and gentle, a harsh contrast to Stephen's ranting.

Becky shook her head.

"Lying whore!"

Becky ignored him. "I don't know why I came tonight," she whispered, tears coating her voice.

"I'll tell you why." Chantelle squatted beside her cousin, her pencil skirt tightening across toned thighs. "It's because Master Cooney is skillful in reading a submissive's body language. Unlike Stephen, who likes to play at being a Dom, Master Cooney knows how to turn a woman on with the gentlest touch, a single whisper—"

"Fucker!"

"—and give her the release her body has been denied her whole adult life."

"I never fucking *denied* her!" Stephen's cheeks mottled, his eyes bugging like a goddamned lunatic on the verge of heartache.

I wouldn't have minded watching his eyes roll back as he dropped dead to the floor.

"Master Cooney is not an abuser using a title to satisfy his own sick desires," Chantelle continued, not paying the Dom wannabe any attention.

"Why you cock-sucking—" Stephen leaped up and took two barreling steps toward Chantelle, arms outstretched.

Titus tackled him from behind.

The two men landed on the carpeted floor with a grunt.

Chantelle didn't flinch as Stephen screamed every explicit word imaginable, promising to kill her. Becky. Me.

"I'll cut your fucking balls off, Cooney, and shove them down your throat!" he screamed.

My brow raised at his outrageous claim, but I didn't reply. Didn't even bother fisting my hands should the fucker get free and attempt to take me out. Titus matched me in size and strength. Stephen didn't stand a chance.

The bouncer yanked Stephen to his feet, both arms behind his back as he continued to spew nonsense.

"Becky," Chantelle said, gaze on her lowered head. "I think it's best for your own safety if you don't go home with Stephen."

"The fuck she won't!" Stephen fought to free himself, but Titus didn't budge.

"Becky?" Chantelle asked for consent to her plan.

Becky hesitated—but nodded.

The breath I hadn't realized I held left in a rush.

"She belongs to me!" Stephen hollered, yanking against Titus's hold. "She's mine and does what *I* say!"

"Not tonight, Stephen." Chantelle stood and turned to finally face him. Her chin tilted up as she stared down at him from the six-foot height her stiletto heels gifted her. "You are going to leave without Becky. You are going to exit this establishment, and if you cause a problem, I'll be more than happy to call the police."

He glared at her but didn't say a word.

"You're both going to have some alone time to calm down. Understood?"

Chantelle nodded toward the door, and Titus dragged Stephen along.

"Becky needs her locker key," I said before they reached the door. "It's in his front pocket."

The bouncer by the door fished the key free from Stephen's pants and handed it to me.

"Titus," Chantelle said without looking away from Becky, "see Stephen to his car and make sure he drives off. If he comes back around, you know what to do."

"It'd be my pleasure. Let's go." Titus pulled Stephen out the door, and the second bouncer followed on his heels, shutting us in quietness.

Chapter 12

Becky

I wanted to sink into the floor and suffocate on the carpet's navy blue fibers. Heat filled my face, and tremors owned my body as I cowered on the chair, arms wrapped around my middle.

Stephen had sounded as though he actually wanted to kill me. He had put me down plenty of times in recent years but never with such vehement passion. He hadn't seemed... right in the head. Overcome by emotions, his better sense had been ruled by reaction.

"Daniel," Chantelle said, breaking into my thoughts, "I would like you to take Becky to my condo."

A tear slid down my cheek as I continued to sit in silence, my entire world crumbling around me.

Chantelle squatted once more beside me and gathered my shaking hands between hers. "You're going to make yourself at home. Food, wine—whatever you desire, help yourself. The guest room is yours for as long as you need it."

I didn't know what I wanted. What I needed...

My mind raced.

How would Stephen react once he got home? What he

would do? My stomach twisted up even tighter as concern for him welled up inside me. He'd never been suicidal even when drinking himself into a stupor over work woes. But would he trash our home? Break all my things? Toss them outside? Go to the police and say my cousin kidnapped me?

"Becky." Chantelle dropped my hands and grasped my face. "Look at me."

I blinked, trying to focus on her concerned eyes.

"You're safe."

Her words didn't register, but I heard them.

"He's not going to touch you again without your permission, do you hear me?"

I nodded, still not processing.

"Daniel is going to drive you to my place where you're going to relax in a hot bath. Sleep for hours. And in the morning, I'll take you over to Stephen's so you can gather some of your stuff."

"I-I'm leaving him?" I asked, pretty sure that was what she suggested.

"Yes." Her tone didn't recommend arguing, but she'd always been a bossy person.

"What about clothes?" More tears welled in my eyes, making the sight of her face look like melting crayons. "I'm like t-twice your size."

"Hardly." She squeezed my hands and appeared to smile. "I have a few items here I can send with you, and like I said, tomorrow we'll gather up some of your things."

I chewed on the inside of my lip, once more contemplating Stephen's reaction and torn over what to do. "I doubt he goes to work tomorrow. He...doesn't do well on his own. Never has. What if he gets drunk and misses work again tomorrow? He's down to his last strike with his boss."

"Stephen is a grown man, Becky," Chantelle said, her voice stern. "He is more than capable of caring for himself."

I wanted to argue but knew she was right. How often had he told me that he didn't need me, that he could just as easily make it on his own? Of course, within an hour, he always apologized.

Used to.

Chantelle pulled me to my feet and hugged me. Some of the tension leaked from me, and I sank against her, seeking strength and comfort since I couldn't seem to find either inside me. "Daniel, will you stay with her until I get home?"

"Of course," he agreed from behind me, his low tone comforting.

"He'll keep you safe," Chantelle assured me. "I trust him with my life, and you can too."

I nodded against her shoulder, breathing deeply to dry my tears. A night away *would* be best. It would give Stephen time to calm down and allow me space to process what had happened to my body while I'd been bound in Master Cooney's ropes.

"Thank you for offering your condo," I said, pulling back and trying for a smile while wiping my cheeks dry of tears. "I've never seen Stephen so angry."

"Can you do me a favor?" Chantelle asked, holding me at arm's length.

I nodded.

"If you're even half tempted to return to him anytime soon, I want you to think about what would have happened if you had gone home with Stephen tonight. Think of the pain and bruises he would inflict. Think of the verbal abuse he would have battered you with."

Swallowing hard, I nodded. Imagining such things wasn't difficult.

"Good." Chantelle released me, and I wrapped my arms around my midsection again. She retrieved her key ring and slid one off, handing it to Master Cooney behind me. "5C. You know which building, right?"

"I do." Master Cooney's deep, quiet voice anchored my mind. I wanted to lean back against him, to soak in his strength, his peacefulness.

Chantelle returned to her chair and moved her mouse around, clicking on her computer a few times. "Titus took Stephen out the front. You parked in the back as usual?" she asked Master Cooney without lifting her gaze from the screen.

"Yes."

She nodded and stood once more, rounding her desk to hug me again. "Everything is going to be okay," she murmured. "I want you to just relax tonight. Unwind and consider your safety in moving forward, okay?"

"Okay." A sigh shuddered over me, and Chantelle released me.

"Now, let's go to the women's locker room and see if we can't find you something a little more appropriate to wear in this cold weather."

ℌℱ

My mind finally lay somewhat quiet while Chantelle rifled through two closets of clothing she kept on hand for emergencies or play. While most pieces were inappropriate for venturing beyond the doors of her kink club, she had a few leggings on hand, one of which fit my fat thighs and ass. A man's 2XL T-shirt covered the rest of me, and I tugged on Stephen's favorite ballet flats and my tattered coat.

Master Cooney waited for us in the reception area. He'd traded in his leather pants for relaxed-fit jeans and a navy Patriots sweatshirt. His gaze slid down over the only coat I owned to my slipper-like shoes, a flicker of a frown denting his brow for a split second.

My face heated, and I turned away.

"Call me when you get there," Chantelle said, giving me another hug my slowly numbing body sank into.

"Will do.

"Get some rest, Becky. I'll be home late, so don't wait up for me."

Home.

My mind went to Stephen again. Was he driving like a maniac? Had he stopped to liquor up like he tended to do when he was upset?

Master Cooney grasped my hand, drawing my mind back to the present. "Ready?" he asked in a soft tone, his eyes warm and kind.

I released a shuddered sigh, pushing aside thoughts of Stephen. He and our issues could wait. I needed to do what Chantelle had said—unwind. Rest. Focusing on my boyfriend from the previous twelve years wouldn't allow either. "Yes."

Master Cooney led me out another door and down a short hallway that ended at a locked exit. With a swipe of a key card, the beep of an unlocking mechanism sounded. Down a flight of stairs, we entered a private parking garage.

I walked in silence—by his side, same as in Chantelle's lounge. Not as a slave, but an equal. Warmth woke in my stomach, and I glanced up at his bulking form.

He smiled down at me, and my belly fluttered.

Whore, Stephen's voice echoed in my memory, and I turned away, a rock replacing the lightness in my center I'd enjoyed for but a moment.

Master Cooney led me to a black SUV and opened the passenger door for me. He waited until I settled and buckled the seatbelt before shutting me inside.

The scent of new leather and his citrus cologne filled my nose. I inhaled deeper, my mind quieting. The rest of my body more alive than what was probably appropriate, considering my circumstances.

He climbed in without a word.

I closed my eyes, breathing deeply as he started the car and pulled out of the garage. What sounded like sleet pelted the windshield, but I didn't have the energy to open my eyes to find out.

We drove in silence, and my mind returned to Master Cooney's rope, his gentle touches, and his kind words without effort. He had called me sweetness. Told me I smelled good. Warmth oozed through my body, settling in my pussy. I shifted on the seat.

I should have been ashamed of my body's reaction to someone other than Stephen, but at that moment, surrounded by his scent, I didn't care. Arousal was an alluring, beautiful thing, the euphoria following a climax a feeling I hoped to experience again someday.

The car slowed, and the sound of sleet stopped. We'd entered another parking garage.

Master Cooney backed into a visitor spot and cut the engine. He hopped out and rounded the front of his car to open my door as I reached for the handle.

"Thank you," I said, climbing from his vehicle.

He took my hand again, and I fought the desire to lean against him, stealing his strength since mine waned. *Thank*

God for elevators, I thought as the overhead ding rang for the fifth time. The doors swished open to a carpeted hallway, cream-colored walls, and soft overhead lighting. A side table with fresh flowers and a handful of paintings gave the hall a warm, homey feel.

5C lay at the end, and Master Cooney let us in without a word. He closed the door behind me while I glanced around. An open-concept living room lay in front of me, with massive windows overlooking Boston's skyline. The kitchen was on the right with stainless steel appliances and granite countertops.

"I'll take your coat," Master Cooney said from behind me.

I unbuttoned and pulled it off my shoulders, but like a real gentleman, he grabbed hold of it and helped me finish.

My throat tightened, and I cursed PMS, Stephen, him cutting me off from the one family member I had left, and my weakness in allowing him to treat me with such disregard. A lick of anger tightened my spine, giving me a sense of strength I hadn't known I possessed.

"Do you want something to drink?" Master Cooney asked, moving into the kitchen.

"Please." I pulled off my slippers.

"Beer? Wine?" He opened the fridge. "OJ, almond milk...cranberry juice."

"Water is fine. Are you going to stay?" I asked as he retrieved one glass.

"I would like to, but I'll go if that's what you prefer." He filled the glass with ice and water from a contraption on the refrigerator's door.

Our fingers brushed as he handed me the glass, and I bit the inside of my lip, shaking my head.

I settled in the living room, the silence of Chantelle's

condo like a soothing balm over my conscience. A clink of ice in another glass sounded, and seconds later, Master Cooney rounded the couch. He hesitated, and I scooted over, hoping he would sit by me rather than in one of the two chairs.

A small smile flitted over my lips as he took me up on the silent offer.

He lifted his tumbler with its amber liquid. "To a night of freedom?" His low voice swept over me, and I shivered.

Oh, the implications that word had on how I had chosen to live my life.

"To freedom," I whispered in return, clinking my glass against his. I swallowed a few gulps as he sipped.

"My father was a lot like Stephen," Master Cooney said, lowering his glass.

I frowned and shifted to face him. "In what way?"

"He was extremely unkind with his words toward my mother." He glanced down at the tumbler all but lost in his large hand. "He was fond of inflicting pain on her too but at least took care to only cause bruises where no one would see them."

I lowered my head, all too aware of the marks he must have noticed the weekend before.

"The relationship between a Dom and his sub is supposed to be one built on trust. Love and acceptance. The only time you should be acting like a slave is if you're sceneing with that intent, and wanting the pleasure you both would find in it."

I sat in silence, considering his words, knowing he spoke the truth I had ignored for far too long. My shoulders sagged with the weight of how off track our relationship had gotten. Stephen hadn't fully grasped the lifestyle he'd thrust us into. Was it too late for him to learn? Could we find our way back to the closeness we used to share?

"What Stephen does to you—" he lowered his voice and angled to face me "— the way he treats you is abuse, Becky. I sat front and center watching a similar relationship for almost my entire childhood."

I clenched my eyes shut, swallowing against the tightness in my throat and chest. "You don't know Stephen like I do," I whispered.

"I've seen the videos." Anger laced his words.

A tear squeezed out between my eyelids and slid down my cheek as I curled in on myself. The way Stephen chose to treat me did not equate to love in any shape or form. I choked on a sob.

Master Cooney's tumbler clinked against the glass-top coffee table, and he took my water from me, also setting it down. He scooted close as another tear escaped, and he pulled me into his arms.

The warmth, the security of his hold broke the dam I'd been forcing my emotions behind since God knew when. I sobbed against his chest, fingers grasping at his sweatshirt, releasing all of the shitty emotions I'd bottled up inside me.

His hands rubbed my back. Warm breath caressed my head. A steady heartbeat sounded in my ear pressed against his rock-hard chest. I wanted to crawl inside him and hide— from myself. From Stephen. From life.

My well ran dry a lot sooner than I expected, but I didn't move from the security of his arms.

"I'm so tired." My voice quaked as I pressed deeper into his hold.

"Sleep."

I breathed him in, filling my lungs, and giving over to the exhaustion pulling on me from every side.

Chapter 13

Daniel

Our time of aftercare had been cut short with traumatic bluntness. I had known Becky would pass the fuck out once feeling safe enough, and rather than moving into a more comfortable position with us both lounging on the couch, I sat still.

Breathing her in.

Touching whatever smooth skin I could reach in a nonsexual way.

Fighting off arousal.

She had climaxed with enough force to snap tension through my ropes—and desperate lust in my balls. They ached, but at least my cock had simmered down to a semi-state of restlessness. I couldn't relive the memory of her flesh being bound, the sight of slickness between her thighs, or the scent of her sweet cream in my nose and on my tongue from when I'd licked my fingers.

Fuck.

Grimacing, I couldn't *not* shift in my seat.

Becky didn't so much as twitch.

A steady exhale deflated my lungs but not my dick. I

had to extract myself from the cuddle position or I was going to lose my ever loving fucking mind...but I didn't wish to disturb Becky.

Teeth gritted to keep curses from spilling, I slowly slid from beneath her body and stood, stretching out stiff muscles.

She lay curled on the couch, her face peaceful in sleep.

She was so goddamned beautiful. Deserved the fucking world for all the shit she'd been dealing with in her life for however many years it had been since Stephen had started the abuse.

I pushed against the violence attempting to rise and tense me up again. Focusing on her comfort and safety, I bent, weaseled my arms beneath her slumbering form, and gently lifted her into my chest.

Heavy breaths continued to escape her parted lips as she hung limp in my hold.

Fuck, she felt good. I wanted to squeeze all her soft flesh. Touch. Lick—

Goddamnit.

Inwardly cursing at myself, I made my way through the short hallway to Chantelle's guest room, which I assumed was the smaller of the two bedrooms. I sat on the edge of the queen-sized bed for balance and reached over to the other to draw back the blankets and top sheet on the opposite side. Cradling Becky once more against me, I straightened, rounded the foot of the bed, and laid her down.

A shuddering sigh rippled through Becky as she rolled on her side, slipping a hand beneath the pillow.

Those damn slipper-like shoes still clung to her feet. She should have better shoes on for the bitter spring weather. Lips in a tight line, I slid the thin things off and set them on the floor. My hands cradled one ankle before I realized I'd reached to touch her again.

My fingers slid downward, noting the sole and pads of her toes were just as soft as the rest of her.

Given the chance, I would massage her arches. Ease soreness or plain old weary muscles from standing all day. I set her foot back on the mattress.

Satisfaction over helping her find peace at least for one night, I tucked her in and stepped back. Dark hair spilled over the white sheets, and equally black eyelashes feathered over the pale skin of her cheeks. Her red lips parted in sleep.

Give Becky blue eyes, and she would have been Snow White come to life. Not as willowy as the cartoon, but I preferred women with full curves. Flesh to bind and hold onto. Softness to lose myself in.

Inwardly cursing yet again, I rubbed a hand over my face before turning away to lower the dimmers. Only a bit of streetlight filtered around through the blinds, keeping me from full blindness.

The couch called to me, but I ignored the right choice. I stretched out on the bed beside Becky—above the blankets, and lay facing her. Call me creepy, but I couldn't help but stare at her in what little light afforded me sight. She lay in shadow, beautiful and still. An angel deserving of love rather than the devil she'd attached herself to.

Somehow, some way, I would show her what freedom tasted like. What it meant to be cherished. Cared for rather than taken advantage of. Her sweet nature needed to be nurtured—not abused.

Closing my eyes, I focused on releasing tension from my body, one muscle at a time. Eventually, I drifted off.

Warmth cradled my side when I roused from sleep.

Darkness still coated the room.

I lay on my back, Becky pressed against my left, the blankets a tangled mess between our waists. Her hand splayed over my stomach and her face rested on my chest. While passed out, we'd become entwined, my arm beneath her shoulders, holding her tight.

Heaven—absolute fucking heaven.

I closed my eyes and soaked in the warmth of her, a sense of rightness welling inside me. I'd cuddled with dozens, hundreds of women in aftercare, but not a single one had gifted me radiating peace through my chest and mind.

Mine.

The word whispered in my head, and following on its heels, a determined desire to protect her settled over me. I'd never been a possessive man, but with Becky?

I released a slow exhale and pulled her in a little closer to me.

She stirred, rubbing her cheek against my chest, her fingers sliding over my right side to hold me tighter. "Master Cooney?" she murmured, her voice barely audible as though she'd spoken in her sleep.

"Daniel," I whispered, caressing her arm and wishing I could hear my real name on her lips.

She sighed and snuggled into me.

Sleep once more came for me, and with it, dreams I had escaped for years.

"Danny—come on!" Mom hollered up the stairwell.

I glanced around my room, not wanting to leave my things, but Mom said we had to hurry. Throat tight, I scampered downstairs, a single backpack slung over my arm.

I didn't know why she had made a sudden decision to leave, what had finally changed Mom's mind about living with my asshole of a father, but I hadn't disagreed when she'd told me to shove some clothes in a bag.

She didn't lock up behind us, just hurried toward the car in the driveway with me cutting through the grass rather than using the walkway like her.

A recognizable rumble barreled down the road an hour earlier than usual.

Mom's footsteps halted. Her face paled, shoulders wilting. She turned toward me, eyes wide. Panic swelled in my chest, and at her whisper for me to run, I told my feet to move.

They didn't.

I stayed rooted like an oak, my stomach in knots.

Dad pulled in behind Mom's car. He climbed from his truck, eyeing the bags in Mom's hands. An ugly shade of red mottled his cheeks. His forehead.

I swallowed hard, having seen the near future too many times to count.

His first swing dropped Mom to her knees, but she knew better than to make a sound. Dad wrapped his hands in her red hair and dragged her toward the house. Her knees scraped on the cement walkway, leaving a trail of red behind her scrambling legs.

Tears welled in my eyes, and I swallowed back a sob, not wanting him to realize I stood in the middle of the yard.

Mom used to beg me to stay silent and tucked me away in a kitchen cabinet when Dad would come home from work angry.

But at thirteen, I'd finally grown too tall to hide.

Her body banged on the stairs leading up to the front porch, and I bit my lip to keep quiet.

Dad hadn't ever laid a hand on me. Not once had I felt the fists he rained down on my mother. His words though had radiated pain through my mind long after the bruises would have faded. As I'd gotten older and taller, Mom had told me to look the other way. Allow Dad to work out his demons on her alone.

How he clung to her afterward, sobbing and begging for forgiveness made me sick. And the fact Mom always gave him grace, held him while he swore he loved her...

Liar.

Anger rose inside me with choking force. My backpack slid to the ground—my feet taking me across red-streaked cement, up wooden stairs, over the threshold through the gaping front door.

Mom whimpered from the kitchen.

Dad cursed her, his voice raised...blaming her actions for his anger, same as always.

I turned the corner, hands fisted at my sides.

He had bound her to a chair. Stood over her, hollering curses, spittle flying from his lips. His shoulders tensed, his arm drawing back, and he let it fly.

Mom's head snapped from the force of his punch, a loud crack hitting my ears as blood flew from her nose. Her eyes rolled up, head tipping forward, and body sagging against the rope holding her to the kitchen chair.

My chest clenched tight, and I bit my lip to keep from sobbing. The taste of iron rushing to coat my tongue.

Dad heaved, ragged breaths hitched his shoulders. He yelled something about her making him do it.

Mom didn't move.

Not one muscle.

The ranting faded, and heavy silence settled over the house like a choking blanket.

"*M-Margo?*" *Dad whispered, dropping to his knees in front of her.* "*Baby?*" *He cradled her chin and lifted her head.*

Mom remained boneless, the middle of her face crushed in from my dad's fat knuckles

"*Margo!*" *Dad screamed, grabbing hold of her neck to keep her head upright. He started blubbering about being sorry—same as fucking always.*

"*No, no, no!*" *he shrieked, feeling along her neck, his bloody fingers shaking while searching...*

For a pulse, I realized.

"*No! I-I didn't mean to...Margo!*"

My heart stopped beating. Ears rang, cutting off his sobs. Numbness settled in my limbs.

Instinct took control over my body—

I gasped, jolting awake.

Jesus fucking Christ.

Swallowing hard, I focused on filling my lungs, calming my racing heart as the memory faded from my mind. Dissolving adrenaline should have made me weak and limp on the bed, but I had to move. Couldn't lay still.

Shifting from beneath Becky's arm, I slid off the mattress. Every inch of my body vibrated as I peered down at her—still in peaceful rest.

I had given her that.

Me.

Daniel Cooney, bondage expert...murderer.

Swallowing hard, I spun on my heel, exited the bedroom, and strode into Chantelle's kitchen. Her purse and keys lay on the table. A quick glance back the hallway showed her bedroom door shut rather than open like it had been the night before when Becky and I had arrived.

Chantelle was there for when Becky woke. She would have someone to talk to, a strong, independent woman to remind her of why she needed to stay away from Stephen. Chantelle would call me if and when they needed me.

Confident Becky was in good hands, I walked out the door and told myself I would give her at least a full day or so with her cousin before pursuing what I wanted.

Becky beside me, tucked close where I would keep her safe for as long as I breathed.

Chapter 14

Becky

The softest sheets and Master Cooney's scent surrounded me.

I stretched and smiled as warmth sprang to life in my core.

Acknowledgment of the arousal I felt and memories from the night before flooded my mind, bringing me fully awake.

I'd slept in Chantelle's guest room, I realized, taking in the warm tones of the walls and blinds attempting to keep out the morning sun. My gaze turned to the wrinkled pillow beside the one I used. The bed smelled like Master Cooney...had he slept beside me?

The desire inside me intensified until I pressed my thighs together to ease my need to be touched.

I couldn't recall walking to the bedroom. Last I remembered, I had curled up against Master Cooney, wishing I could crawl beneath his skin and hide from reality. He had held me while I'd cried, and I'd experienced true comfort for the first time in years.

He must have carried me into the bedroom.

"Oh, God." Heat rose to my cheeks as I sagged into the mattress.

I hoped he hadn't thrown out his back. I remembered him pulling my rope-wrapped body off the floor at Chantelle's when I'd been on the verge of flying into oblivion. The man was a pure mountain of muscle, but stringing me up—and carrying me to the bedroom—couldn't have been an easy feat.

A knock sounded, sending a rush of adrenaline to my heart.

The door cracked open, and Chantelle stuck her head in before I could squeak.

Not Master Cooney. Bummer.

"Good, you're awake," my cousin said, walking in with two cups of coffee in her hands. A green silk dressing gown hung past her knees. No makeup and a messy bun made her look like any other woman rather than an intimidating, glamorous Domme. She moved unlike a typical woman, though. Confidence—some sort of authoritative air—followed her like it did Master Cooney, immediately setting me at ease.

I sat up and leaned against the headboard as she crossed the room and settled onto the bed beside me.

She handed me a cup of coffee and smiled. "How'd you sleep?"

"Like the dead."

"Good." She sipped, her gaze resting on my face as I lifted the mug to my lips and blew the steam over the rim. "How long did Daniel stay?"

"Daniel...Master Cooney?"

"He should only be Master Cooney to you while in a scene," she said, a small smile at the corner of her lips.

Daniel. The name fit and also stirred that need inside

me again. But her question meant he had left. Once again, disappointment slid through my veins.

"I-I don't know," I replied, trying to keep my voice from sounding whiny.

"You enjoyed acting as his sub last night, didn't you?"

Heat rushed to my face even as my stomach twisted over my body's reaction to someone other than Stephen. "Very much," I answered honestly regardless of the guilt wanting to control me.

"He's the perfect man for you." Chantelle sounded nonchalant, but I could tell by her calculating gaze something brewed in her brain.

I didn't comment, allowing her center stage to say whatever she thought I needed to hear.

"You're a true submissive in every way, and he's a gentle dominant uninterested in inflicting pain."

An ache spread through my chest at the memory of his kindness and soothing touches. Sipping my coffee, I remained silent, the unrest of desire and shame swirling through my thoughts.

Chantelle huffed an exhale. "Aren't you tired of the abuse, Becky? Stephen isn't going to 'get better'," she said, adding the quotes around the words I used to claim weekly back before he'd cut me off from my cousin. "He's spiraling out of control to the point where I'm starting to fear for your life."

"How would you know that? You and I haven't spoken in months," I murmured.

"And whose fault is that?" she snapped. "To answer your question, I've seen the latest videos he uploaded, and quite honestly, I'm surprised the websites he's posted to hasn't removed them. He's an asshole, not a Dom. Stephen is nothing but a selfish prick who gets off on hurting and humiliating you."

My throat grew tight, and I lowered my head, unable to argue in defense of the man he'd morphed into the previous couple of years.

"His actions toward you are not born of *love*," Chantelle pressed, and I could hear the scowl in her voice. "They're from of a sick mind who needs serious help—beyond what you being a slave to him will *ever* help heal."

My vision hazed as tears welled in my eyes. She didn't lie, but I couldn't stop trying. "He's all I've ever known, the only man who has ever shown an interest in me—"

"Bullshit."

I met her hard gaze, wondering what planet she thought we walked on.

"*Daniel* got hard as fuck while tying you up in his ropes."

An unsteady inhale filled my lungs as I got ahold of my emotions. "That was during a session in your BDSM club. A scene. Nothing more."

"Remember the way he looked at you? The way he touched you?" She leaned toward me, gaze intense. "The words he said to you...*so beautiful. So soft. My sweetness.* That's not just a man playing a role, Becky."

Warmth filled me as his voice echoed in my memory. "H-how do you know what he said to me?"

"I have cameras and mics throughout the club, sending live feed to my computer," she stated without apology.

I shifted on the soft mattress beneath me, heat once more rushing to my face. "You watched him tie me up?"

"I also saw him lift you off the ground without effort and set you soaring. I heard you climax for the first time, free as a fucking butterfly while bound by him."

My throat tightened again, keeping embarrassment at bay. He had sent me into subspace, also something Stephen had never managed to do.

"Daniel wants you, but he's a gentleman and won't say or do anything until you make the decision to leave Stephen and start your life over."

Her declaration took a while to compute...but I couldn't begin to imagine she spoke the truth.

"Why—how..." I pinched the bridge of my nose. "What makes you think that?" I asked once I gathered my thoughts.

"He told me."

I slumped against the pillow behind me, my body deflating even as my heart rate accelerated. "No."

"Oh, yes." That sly grin I'd grown wary of when we were little kids lifted her Botoxed, plump lips.

A lightbulb went off in my brain, and I suddenly knew my cousin had instigated the entire event that had led us to that point. The giveaway Stephen had never entered. The prize of a two-night pass to her BDSM club. The knowledge that Stephen would offer me up as a volunteer because he was just that arrogant.

All to point out what I had been aware of but ignored—Stephen had crossed over lines while taking me through scenes. The power dynamic he denied that Master Cooney had made known to me the first night he'd tied me up on stage.

"You want me to leave Stephen, don't you?" She'd never thought Stephen was good enough for me...and she'd taken his ignorance of the real lifestyle to make him appear like a fool. More than a little anger stirred inside me at her actions, but I withheld from lashing out.

"Yes. And, when Daniel comes back around to pursue you—and he *will*—I pray to God you'll be wise enough to hold onto him and never let go. He's a rare one, Becky. The type dreamers dream of. The kind of man women wished whispered poetry in their ears."

"Why don't you claim him, then?" I asked, frowning, not sure how to handle my loyalty to the man who had loved me for twelve years and my manipulative cousin.

She huffed a snort of laughter. "Because I like to dominate men. Tie them up and inflict the kind of pain that turns me and a submissive on. Daniel wouldn't let me touch him with a crop let alone my lips."

The thought of Chantelle strapping Daniel to a cross and hurting him tightened my stomach. "Would you?" I asked. "I mean if he agreed to submit to you?"

"No," she answered without hesitation. "I prefer blonds with a little less...breadth of chest and shoulder width."

"I happen to like his size," I murmured the thought as it flitted through my mind. "He makes me feel safe."

"He'll *keep* you safe if you let him," Chantelle whispered back with a sure smile.

I studied the mug clasped between my hands. "But what about Stephen?"

"What about him?"

"I've spent almost half my life as his girlfriend. Leaving him isn't...I-I don't think he would react in a healthy way."

"He'll probably throw a major hissy like the little pansy he is, but other than that, starting over would be a breeze. There's no marriage, so no divorce. It's simply a matter of packing up your shit and moving out."

I chewed on the inside of my lip. She made it sound so simple, but my life was tied to his. Bound up tight in years of shared history. "He wouldn't let me go so easily."

"He wouldn't have a choice, and if he does come after

you, call the cops. File a restraining order. Find yourself a real man who will protect you from him."

I smiled at her naivety. "That's a fairytale happily ever after."

"It's yours to take."

She sounded so confident in her statement, but my smile faded as I was too well-acquainted with reality to imagine such an ending for me. "I can't just give up and walk away on him, Chantelle. All of those years I spent investing in his life, his mental and emotional health...he doesn't mean to hurt me. It's just that stress pulls him under. He gets overwhelmed and needs someone to help with the demons haunting his mind."

"That someone is a goddamned shrink, not *you*."

"He *needs* me," I reiterated, thinking of Stephen's tears, and the countless sobs he had released on my shoulders over the years. He'd gotten so sick...

Chantelle stared at me, lips pursed, her gaze full of concern. "You've always made excuses for him."

"They're not excuses. They're reasons for our behavior, and we all have them. Don't pretend you don't." I stared her down for a change, hoping she remembered why she'd striven to become a Domme.

She didn't bat an eyelash. "You're going to go back to him, aren't you? Even though he threatened to kill you for your betrayal."

"I didn't betray him," I whispered. "My body did."

"No." Chantelle climbed off the bed and glared down at me. "You responded to the gentle touch of a loving man, one who turns you on because you feel a connection to him."

I opened my mouth to argue I had a connection with *Stephen.* Our lives were intertwined to the root of us, yes, but did I actually experience more than a nurturing draw toward him? I came up empty and pressed my lips together. Was that why I'd never climaxed with him? Didn't feel arousal from his touch? Damned tears made my vision watery again. "I-I don't know what to do."

Chantelle heaved a sigh. "You're staying here until you do."

I glanced down at the wrinkled T-shirt and leggings she'd let me borrow the night before. "I don't have any of my clothes."

"Get out of bed," my cousin ordered. "Shower and ready to take a drive by Stephen's house. We'll pick up some of your things and come back here for a little girl time."

"What if he's home?"

"This is his weekend to work."

"What—how do you know that?" I asked, my brow furrowing.

A coy smile lifted her lips. "He forbade you from speaking to me, but that doesn't mean I haven't been keeping tabs on your life, Becky. *Both* your lives."

"*That's* not creepy," I muttered.

"It's called protective instincts. Now, get up. Let's get shit done so we can share a bottle of wine and celebrate your freedom."

Unsure of what to do outside of obeying her command, I slid off her soft mattress, slipped on the ballet flats that lay on the floor, and followed her into the hallway.

Chantelle's confidence, her sure plan of attack carried me through readying for the day and eating a full breakfast along with another cup of coffee.

And when we drove westward away from the city?

I chewed on my fingernails, torn over hating what Stephen did to me—and yet wanting to help bring him back from the darkness he'd tumbled into.

Chapter 15

Daniel

My heart bottomed out at Chantelle's words. I stumbled back into Micah's living room, sure I'd heard her wrong. "She what?"

"I know," Chantelle said over the cell I had clasped to my ear. "I'm pissed she changed her mind and decided to go back, but there was nothing I could do."

"Fuck." Eyes closing, I dropped onto the couch, the beer I had retrieved from Micah's fridge wrapped in my fist.

"She'd really seemed to listen to me Saturday morning though, when I was giving it to her straight, and agreed to retrieve some of her clothes. She drove her car to my place and spent the night again but woke up this morning determined to make things right with him. She left around noon," Chantelle said.

I opened my eyes and stared at the huge flat-screen hanging in Micah's man cave. The Celtics were down by 26, but I didn't give two shits about basketball at that moment. Stephen had been livid Friday night—on a goddamned murderous rampage in his mind. The shit that had come out of his mouth...

"Was he at the house when you took her over there yesterday?" I asked, my blood heated even as fear for Becky slithered goose bumps over my nape.

"No."

"Fuck." I scrubbed a hand down over my face, adrenaline rushing through me. "Think he's going to hurt her?"

"I pray to God he doesn't, or I'll make sure he disappears never to be found again."

I didn't doubt Chantelle's declaration one bit. She would take his life, burn his body, and feed his ashes to the ocean without a second thought. "Just make sure you string him up for a bit and make him suffer," I muttered. "Better yet, let me help."

"Our hands are tied right now, but at least Becky knows she has a safe place to go when she finally realizes the truth of her situation. I told her if she doesn't check in with me within twenty-four hours, I'll drive by myself."

Better than fucking nothing, but the entire situation made me antsy. Fucked with my head and twisted my insides up tight. "Keep me informed, will you?"

"Of course."

"And if there's anything I can do, anything she needs..."

"I'll call you first," Chantelle promised, her voice soft for a change.

"Thanks." I hung up and tossed my cell onto the end table beside me. Four sets of eyes stared at me.

Blake, Reid, and Jarod were all former Elites and my good friends who rarely got together without women or children in tow. Reid and Jarod could have been brothers with their matching tall, dark, and handsome looks, but it was Micah's blue-eyed gaze that caught mine.

He lounged in his favorite recliner, brow raised.

"I'm quitting Elite," I stated without preamble or hesitation.

His eyes narrowed, facial expression hardening as he scoffed and glanced around at the other employees he'd lost to love. "Some woman grab you by the balls too?" he asked, giving me his full focus once more.

"She hasn't touched me yet. Has no clue she's mine."

He swigged his beer and muted the Celtics game without taking his focus off me. None of the other guys made a noise of complaint. "Explain."

I gave my friends the brief version, sticking to the facts, but it still took me a good twenty minutes to get through sharing what had happened in the previous nine days. Micah was the only guy there involved in the BDSM lifestyle and knew who Chantelle was. He didn't seem surprised by her cunning ways and what she'd set into motion.

He sat quietly after I finished, and I swallowed down the last of my beer. "I know from experience that she won't be forced into leaving him," I tacked on.

I hadn't told anyone except Chantelle about my parents, but even she didn't know the whole story. Only those in my past were aware of what had happened that hot August morning. Meeting each of the four men's stares made me realize I wouldn't be judged by them. Wouldn't be pitied for what I'd endured. They needed to understand my first-hand knowledge of the situation Becky was in.

"My dad was an abusive asshole," I stated, my voice steadier than I'd expected. "My mom stayed too long—and I got to witness what that cost her. So yeah, I'm well acquainted with the shit Becky is going through, and I'm powerless to make her see she deserves better than that fucker."

"Shit," Jarod muttered, shaking his head. His dark eyes bored into me as though reading the inner turmoil I sometimes had to face when memories riled up on the offense. "You okay?"

"I got over that shit," I stated a half-truth considering the dream I'd had Friday night, "but this situation is definitely dragging my past back up."

"We're here if you need us," Blake stated firmly, his stare intense. "Whatever it is, we got your back."

"I could call Uncle Sully if you want?" Reid suggested, his tone and demeanor just as serious as the others.

Chief of Police Sullivan had helped him and Jessie out when her ex had come sniffing around, intent on making her pay for putting him behind bars.

"I appreciate it, but I can't do anything until Becky changes her mind and decides on her own to leave."

"So what the fuck are we gonna do?" Jarod asked, leaning forward from where he sat on the couch to my left, elbows on knees. "Just sit around and twiddle our thumbs?"

My chest went tight at how the four men supported me when we had only been friends for around a year.

"I know some people," Blake tossed out with a shrug while sprawling out over the couch's corner in his usual air of arrogance—confidence, he would say.

I huffed a snort. With his connections thanks to his grandfather being a senator and in the country's one percent of rich pricks, I didn't doubt Blake's words. There had been more than one rumor on social media over the years about the senator and one of the mafia families from North End.

"You could kidnap her and whisk her away to my place down in Cancun," Micah offered.

"You can use my family's private jet," Blake tacked on.

"I have access to drugs at the hospital that would knock her out if you think she'd fight."

My gaze swung toward Jarod at his suggestion.

"What?" he asked, glancing around at the rest of the guys. "Just because I'm a nurse means I can't do unethical things for the right reasons?"

I shook my head and released a slow exhale. "While I appreciate all the offers, I won't cross lines. Can't have Becky years down the road deciding I coerced her into a new life. She's got to figure this shit out on her own."

"Be her friend."

Brow raised, I peered over at Reid on the second recliner.

He studied me with dark eyes as though trying to figure out exactly how far I *would* go to win her affection. "Find out where she goes when she isn't with Stephen," he continued. "Make sure you're there. It might take you a long-ass time," he said, getting up from his chair, "but show her what a real man is. Anyone else need another beer?"

Micah and Blake declined, but Jarod agreed.

"I think Reid is onto something," Micah said as our friend traipsed toward the kitchen.

"It's how he won over Jessie," Blake said before swallowing down some of his lager.

"Didn't you do the same?" I asked.

Blake grinned. "I was friendly, but I also pursued the fuck out of my little Birdie. Took four attempts to get Wren to say yes to me and everything I had planned for her."

Reid returned, gave Jarod his drink, and once more sat.

"How did you win over Christine?" I asked Jarod.

"Fucked the memory of every other man and dick from her mind."

Reid snorted on his mouthful of beer, some droplets spewing from between his lips.

"Watch the furniture!" Micah barked.

"Fucking hell," Reid muttered and coughed, wiping at his T-shirt.

Jarod snickered. "Seriously though, it was when we were buried beneath that rubble that Christine realized we were meant to be together."

He had cared for her. Hadn't given up hope. Believed they would be rescued and had done everything in his power to keep her alive until a shot of light split the darkness they'd been trapped inside.

"Whatever you do," Blake said, "don't give up."

"She knows the safeword you gave her," Micah added. "Trust her to use it if she wants you to stop."

"Offer her a friendly massage," Reid said with a one-shoulder shrug. "You get your hands on her, and she learns what genuine concern looks and feels like."

I'd heard the story about the night he'd first met Jessie and she hadn't taken advantage of Elite's offer of his dick. He'd rubbed her down instead, making her come then pass out on the hotel bed where she got to spend the night without interruption from her toddler daughter.

Friends. I could do that. With or without benefits—I would take whatever I could get. And I would show her exactly how a woman ought to be treated.

I grabbed my phone. Relaxing once more back on the couch, I stretched my legs out and hit redial.

"Chantelle," I said after she answered. "I've got an idea."

"*My* idea!" Reid hollered so she would hear him.

"I'm all ears," she said.

Chapter 16

Becky

Stephen had seemed surprised to find me home on Sunday when he got home from work—but one blink returned the rage I'd witnessed Friday night. His fist connected with my jaw, sending me stumbling back against the counter.

I'd blubbered something about being sorry, and seconds later, he dropped to where I'd slumped on the kitchen floor. Tears had filled his eyes, agony radiating from deep inside him. For the first time in months, he brushed aside my apology and offered one of his own.

He'd held me. Sobbed. Begged me to forgive him, to never leave him. He would be lost without me. Wouldn't survive on his own.

Even though my face had ached, my heart broke for him.

Promises to be a better man and partner poured from his lips, most of which I'd heard before. I wanted to believe him.

I chose him. The life we'd built together. His mental health in knowing mine might have to suffer a bit longer before he healed. Usually, I kept my mouth shut when we discussed his inner demons, but after a full day with my cousin, I felt a little more confident in speaking my mind. I suggested he see a therapist. Maybe go to an AA meeting.

Surprisingly, he agreed to both.

Anything, he'd said, to make things right between us again.

He'd tried to make love to me that night, but my body refused to become aroused. Rather than getting angry, he continued to pet and kiss me while finishing.

Once Stephen slept, I'd cried. I thought I'd made the right decision, but my heart hurt. For more. Just a hint of what I'd experienced while bound for Master Cooney. Thoughts of him had crept in while Stephen attempted to make me feel good, and shame had crashed through my brain like a ten-car pile-up.

I was nothing but a cheating whore.

Monday, guilt and determination lay heavily on my mind, and I asked Stephen to spend the day with me since he had off work.

While in the bathroom with the door locked, I secretly shot a text to Chantelle's new cell number letting her know I was fine—that I couldn't talk because Stephen waited for me.

She had given me a new phone number since Stephen knew her old one and often browsed through my cell. I'd saved her as "Library" in my contacts since he wouldn't think anything of it if he felt the need to poke around in my personal stuff again.

I turned off my phone to keep any pinged notifications from drawing Stephen's attention.

Bundled up, we walked on the beach hand in hand, breathing in the brisk spring air, listening to rhythmic waves crashing on the shore. We visited our favorite sub shop and shared a steak bomb for lunch. The afternoon wasted away with us on the couch, watching his favorite home improvement show. I cooked him a pork roast and mashed potatoes, one of his favorite meals, and he simply wrapped his body around mine as we once more lay in bed.

He nuzzled my neck. Whispered in my ear that he loved me and appreciated my loyalty to staying with him. Again, he reminded me that he wouldn't survive without me by his side.

Tears slid down my cheeks as I lay beneath the weight of his heavy arm over my chest. I felt...trapped both physically and emotionally. Held in place by history and manipulation I hadn't considered the truth of before talking with Chantelle.

She'd told me about narcissism, and the traits matched Stephen to a T. But I still struggled with the sense of being tied to him for so long. Responsible in some way for his mental health.

Perhaps things would get better once he started speaking to the therapist. I'd called around earlier in the day, finding someone local who accepted his insurance and could meet with him by teleconference.

His appointment was on the following afternoon after he got off work, and a little inkling of hope resided in my heart.

I'd gathered up the AA information and had given it to him that night after dinner. He'd agreed to call the number I'd written down the next day during his lunch break.

Tuesday morning, I made Stephen's lunch and sent him to work, his *I love you* in my ears, the press of his lips on my bruised jaw lingering long after he left.

I powered up my cell to find Chantelle had texted a half

dozen times in the previous twenty-four hours since I'd reached out to her. I'd been smart to shut my phone off.

Me: **I'm doing well.**

While my response wasn't exactly a lie, it *felt* like one. I wasn't sure I trusted my own emotions, and I hated how my entire life had been called into question by my cousin's meddling. Yet some part of me appreciated what she'd attempted to point out.

Was she right?

Wrong?

How was I supposed to know the truth of my situation or my heart? Conflicting desires roused up anxiety, and after less than two days at home, I was exhausted.

Library: **Can you call me?**

My heart rate picked up at the knowledge she would weasel every detail out of me. That included the purplish hue on the left side of my jaw.

Fingers shaking, I typed out my reply. **I have to get ready for work.**

Library: **Did he hurt you?**

I chewed on my inner lip before replying, **He made love to me without cruelty in any form.**

It wasn't until I hopped out of the shower and dressed that Chantelle replied.

Library: **If you need anything—ANYTHING AT ALL—I don't care what time it is or where you are. Call me.**

Tears pricked my eyes, and my throat swelled.

Me: **I will.**

Feeling somewhat buoyed, I took my old clunker to the coffee shop where I'd been working part-time for six months. I used to have shifts at the Dunks a few blocks from home, but I'd been fired. For five years, I hadn't missed a single day regardless of the soreness I experienced after sceneing with him. Stephen had said my loyalty should have earned me the manager's position they'd hired someone with lesser experience to fill. He'd gone off the rails, shown up while I was working for the new manager, and created such a ruckus on my behalf that I'd left on the spot, my head hung in shame.

The official phone call from the owner stating I didn't need to finish out the week's schedule had come two hours later.

I did as Stephen suggested and started at the bottom of the totem pole once more, pouring coffee and toasting bagels for a privately owned business. But I enjoyed the mindless job, causing smiles to lift lips by handing over the nectar of the gods and quick breakfasts that helped people get through their day.

I had no lofty goals, no desire to rise in the ranks and run a shop of my own as Stephen pushed for. The idea of being in charge made me want to cringe. I couldn't imagine having to be the one employees came to with grievances or having to listen to pissed-off customers and somehow make things right for however they felt wronged.

Laboring behind the scenes had always been my preference.

I'd been the shy girl hiding in the back of class, the one who never raised her hand and barely managed to squeak out answers if called on. While insecurities from my childhood still affected me in adulthood, I'd gained a little confidence in knowing I excelled at making people happy.

Cleaning up spills even when they hadn't been mine and no one asked for me to do so. Agreeing to cover others' shifts if they were in a bind. Taking on the task of bathroom checks since my fellow employees despised doing so. Stephen claimed I allowed others to take advantage of me, and it pissed him off, so I stopped telling him about the good deeds I did.

I cradled the pleasant feelings in my chest from having done them, knowing I chose right in helping others out.

Tuesday, two hours into my shift, one of the high schoolers who worked with me complained she wasn't well and asked to go home. One of her friends had stopped in a little earlier, quietly telling her about a party, asking if she could cut out early and go along.

I'd overheard the conversation but kept my mouth shut when our manager allowed her to leave before her scheduled time. Instead, I remembered what it was like to be a teen with no friends outside of Stephen. I wanted the girl to live while she had the chance, to experience all life had to offer.

I agreed to cover the rest of her shift, which meant staying two extra hours.

Knowing Stephen would be pissed I wouldn't be home to make his dinner, I texted while on break rather than calling, promising to pick up a pizza on the way home. Meat lovers, his favorite. His reply of **Fine** didn't clue me in on his mood or real thoughts, but at least he hadn't left a tirade or called to ream me out like he usually would when angry.

Perhaps he really had turned the page in the book of his life, and a semi-happily ever after could be had for the two of us.

Heaving a heavy sigh of relief, I tucked my cell away and went back to work with a smile on my face.

Chapter 17

Daniel

I told myself to lay low on the friendship plan, let Stephen calm the fuck down, and give Becky some breathing space. Chantelle had texted me a few times to let me know he hadn't assaulted her, but I lasted all of two days before heading into the coffee shop she worked at.

The need to see her face and make sure for myself she wasn't hurting had me driving westward over my lunch break.

My height made it easy to see over the counter.

Becky had her back to me, tossing a sliced bagel into the toaster.

"Large regular," I told the cashier, keeping my gaze on Becky.

She tilted her head and glanced at the screen of orders beside her, and I saw fucking red.

The makeup she'd slathered on didn't hide the bruise along her jaw that hadn't been there on Saturday in the early morning hours when I'd watched her sleep.

Motherfucker.

I took my coffee and stepped toward the left. Forcing

my anger down, I put on what I hoped was a pleasant expression. "Becky?"

She stiffened and turned. A slow smile lit her features, making her dark eyes sparkle.

I swallowed hard. She was so goddamned beautiful.

"D-Daniel!" With a quick glance from side to side, she moved toward the counter separating us. "What are you doing here?"

I lifted my coffee, my grin coming easy. "Needed an afternoon fix and was in the area. It's really good to see you," I said, trailing my gaze over the rest of her face. No other bruises marred her smooth skin.

"Y-you, too." Her smile wobbled.

"Your cousin told me you went home on Sunday."

Becky glanced down and shifted on her feet as though ashamed—of her actions or perhaps Stephen's? Anger clenched my guts, twisting my stomach up tight. "I did."

"Is everything okay?" I managed to keep my tone light.

"It will be." She lifted her head and tried for another smile but failed. "I...uh...have to get to work. I'll see you around?"

"Absolutely," I assured her since hope had laced her words. I didn't move until she turned her back once more and grabbed the toasted bagel from the tray. She didn't glance my way as I left.

Twice more that week, I drove from the office to get coffee from a shop a half hour farther northeast than the Dunks a quarter mile down the street. Both times, I caught her eye, shared a smile and a few quick words.

She assured me that Stephen was doing well. Had spoken with a therapist and was starting to attend AA meetings. Our interactions were better than nothing, especially since the final time earned me the knowledge of when she got to go on break.

The following week, I showed up five minutes before that time, ordered my coffee, and sat in one of the leather chairs by the gas fireplace rather than going back to the office. She passed me on the way to the bathroom, but I waved her over when she came out.

"Are you allowed to take your break out here?" I asked, motioning toward the empty chair beside me.

"I could." Lower lip between her teeth, she checked out the patrons lingering around the shop.

"Afraid Stephen will find out?" I asked, recognizing the hitch of her shoulders.

Her dark eyes peered into mine as though trying to figure out what I was up to. She eventually nodded.

"He doesn't like you having friends," I stated what I expected to be true.

"Not of the male variety, no," Becky replied, her voice low. "Especially one who...well..." Her cheeks turned a deep pink. "You know."

I raised a brow along with a corner of my mouth. Yeah, I knew all right. The memory of her cries while climaxing still haunted my dreams—day and night alike. I longed to hear them again, but with my cock buried deep inside of her lush body. "Yeah." I cleared my throat, needing to adjust my swelling dick. "Understandable."

Her blush darkened, and she wrung her hands at her waist. "Why are you here, Master Cooney?"

Fuck.

I bit back a groan. That title on her lips made me hard as fuck. I glanced around as well before returning my attention to her face. "Call me Daniel."

"Daniel." She smiled, my name escaping her mouth with breathlessness even worse. "Okay."

"Save Master and Sir for when we're sceneing."

Her smile faded, her pupils dilated, and her pouty lips parted.

So much for keeping things friendly. I stood and moved into her personal space so she had to tip her head or move away. She chose the first. Allowing my desire for her to show in my gaze, I peered down at her, my fingers itching to touch. "I can't wait to hear you call me both again someday."

"I-I'm with Stephen," she whispered, taking that step back I'd expected.

"You deserve so much more, Becky," I said, my voice low. "Someone who will care for you. Love you in the way you deserve."

"W-What are you saying?" Her voice escaped breathless with desire.

"I'm telling you that I could be that man—if you'd let me." I pulled a business card from my pocket with my cell and address written on the back. "If you ever need anything —anything at all, day or night—call me. Please."

Becky accepted my card with a shaky hand and glanced down at it. "Thank you." Tears glistened in her eyes when she lifted her gaze, her dark eyes riotous with conflicting emotions.

I wanted to wrap her up in my arms and assure her that I could protect her from everyone and everything. "Even if you decide to stay with Stephen," I murmured, "I'll always be here for you, Becky. I'll be your friend, just a phone call away. Don't ever forget that."

"I-I won't."

I turned and strode out of the shop before I did something I regretted like haul her into my arms without consent and kiss her senseless.

While I doubted she would ever just up and leave Stephen because some other man claimed to want her, I hoped like hell it wouldn't take something drastic to make up her mind. No new bruises tinged her visible skin, but that only made me fear what lay beneath her clothing.

Too often, Dad had made sure Mom's pretty face remained unmarred so as not to attract attention. But *I* had paid attention. The lifting of arms had pulled up Mom's shirt, revealing an inch or two of discoloration. Winces lined her face whenever she'd bent to retrieve whatever shit she'd needed. Pain had etched her forehead when she would gingerly sit on the wooden chairs at suppertime.

The vivid and haunting memories stayed with me for the next couple of hours, and I found myself leaving the office early and driving back to the coffee shop. I parked in the gas station lot across the street a few minutes before Becky left.

She exited the building and climbed into a beat-up, old Chevrolet without glancing in my direction. I followed her at a safe distance and ten minutes later studied the shack-like house she disappeared into.

A broken concrete slab acted as a stoop, chipped white-and-yellow paint peeled from the curled wooden siding. A sagging roofline suggested major structural issues, and plywood covered a few of the windows. The house should have been condemned.

I heaved a heavy sigh, thinking of my own single-family home in a much nicer town northwest of Boston. Brand new construction to my specifications. High-end everything to make for a greener and more comfortable life. The thought of Becky in my personal space sent a strange tingle through my chest, far from unpleasant—definitely addictive. I wanted to share it all with her.

How or why I'd come to that conclusion so quickly, I didn't know. I didn't believe in love at first—or third—sight. But Becky? She was purely sweet smiles with a humble spirit, perfectly submissive, and all woman in the best ways physically possible.

Fuck.

I groaned but, already feeling like a major stalker, gripped my steering wheel to keep from stroking myself through my slacks.

I needed to embedded her fully into my life. Fear of Stephen would keep her from meeting with me in public though, so what option did I have other than to check in on her at work now and then?

Something had to give because I was running out of patience—and feared another meltdown on Stephen's part that would leave Becky a battered mess.

If she survived at all.

Chapter 18

Becky

Daniel continued to stop by every few days for a coffee and a quick chat. At least twice a week he showed up around my break time, and I lingered a few minutes to speak with him. I wanted to sit beside him and soak in his peaceful aura to steady my own, but I knew better.

Somehow, some way, Stephen would find out.

It didn't help that he'd been declining after only a few days of doing well. He told me he'd spoken with the therapist twice but felt it was nothing but a waste of time. He claimed to have gone to an AA meeting.

I wasn't sure I believed him.

He got in trouble again at work, and while I listened to his ranting about his asshole boss who was the real problem, I didn't ask questions in an attempt to get to the truth of what had gone down.

Another week went by, and his complaints turned to the bills piling on the kitchen counter. My dry cunt once more became an issue. He called me names and degraded me while creating new content for that damned website he uploaded videos.

I had hoped that a taste of the kink club and seeing how other Doms behaved would have been a positive influence on Stephen, but his behavior didn't change while sceneing. I wasn't allowed a safeword since I ought to trust him to know my limits after being together for twelve years. It didn't matter that I begged him for a break and didn't climax for him.

Stephen didn't stop until *he* was done.

I neared the end of my rope emotionally and finally reached out to Chantelle via text for advice. Doing so earned me a voicemail—an earful on leaving and starting over. She also mentioned Daniel the one time I called her in tears.

But the same as always, I calmed while on the phone with her, reasoned away Stephen's actions, and focused on striving to better things for him, for us.

I couldn't rid my mind of the memory of Daniel and his kind, dark eyes though. I dreamed of him touching me, kissing me, bringing me to climax again. Twice, I woke aroused and slipped quickly from bed before Stephen stirred.

Emotional exhaustion bruised the skin beneath my eyes more than Stephen ever had. I binged on ice cream and hot fudge. Gained almost five pounds the week after I learned Stephen had begun drinking again.

If he'd ever quit at all.

Good old Jack Daniels became his best friend as I spiraled into despair alongside him. I was a fading flower in the forgotten garden of life but couldn't find the strength inside myself to leave the only life I knew. Atop Stephen's manipulations to keep me by his side, I battled insecurity.

I stayed long after I should have escaped regardless of my inability to support myself.

A month after I climaxed for the first time from a mere brush of Daniel's fingertips, Stephen lost his job.

I answered his call, having no clue about his mood.

"Take a bottle of JD to the playroom," he hissed the order rather than returning my greeting. "I want you on your hands and knees, the booze between your spread thighs."

I licked my suddenly dry lips as my stomach twisted. Adrenaline raced through my system, making me shake. He'd never held such venom in his voice, threatening danger that slid shivers down my spine. "W-What happened?"

"I lost my job, and we're going to celebrate so I don't get tempted to blow my goddamned brains all over the bedroom wall."

Shit.

I gulped audibly.

"Don't even *think* about going anywhere. You better be waiting for me exactly as I told you, or I swear to God, Becky..." His voice trailed off, but I got the message loud and clear.

He hung up, and I stared at the phone in the sudden silence.

If I didn't do something, he would eventually kill me. I'd heard that truth in his words, the same thing Chantelle had told me time and again.

And I wasn't ready to die.

My heart a deadened weight in my chest, I dumped all of the alcohol I could find down the drain. Sitting down at the kitchen table, I clenched my hands in my lap to keep them from shaking. For the first time, I had outright defied his orders, but with his income gone, we would need to figure out a plan for our future. Trying to work out his aggression on me and drinking until he dropped wouldn't accomplish a single thing.

The click of the lock jolted me in my chair, and I bit my tongue to keep from whimpering.

Stephen's footsteps squeaked on loose floorboards in the entryway.

"I'm in the kitchen," I called out, my voice betraying my fear.

He stalked through the archway a few seconds later, a thunderous scowl denting his forehead. Eyes red-rimmed let me know he'd already been at the bottle.

"The fuck you doing up here? Thought I told you to go down to the playroom?"

"We n-need to talk." My voice shook along with my insides.

"Talk, talk, talk." He rolled his eyes and stomped across the kitchen. "That's all you fucking do is *talk!*" he lied and grabbed hold of my hair to jerk my head back.

Tears sprang to life in my eyes, and I bit my tongue to keep from crying out, which would only turn him on.

"You were to wait for me downstairs like a good little fucking whore, but no. You *had* to disobey and piss me off." Stephen yanked me from the chair and onto the floor. I landed hard on my knees and bit my lip until I tasted blood "Now, you're going to pay."

I grasped his wrist to stop him from yanking my hair out, and he glanced at the counter where three empty liquor bottles sat.

"The fuck!" he shrieked, pushing my face into the side of the table.

The impact jarred my head, and stars dotted my vision.

Tears streamed unbidden, and I slumped onto the floor, my cheek throbbing with my heartbeat as he walked to the counter.

He upended each bottle, cursing when nothing more than a drip splattered on the countertop. "You fucking bitch!"

I curled into a ball as he pulled back his leg. His boot thumped against my lower back, and I cried out again at the pain knifing through me.

"That's every bottle I had in this damn house!" He kicked again, landing a blow to my left shoulder blade. Another harsh pull on my hair uncurled my body and tipped my head back. My heart tried to beat through my chest bone as I struggled to keep quiet. "I'm going to the liquor store, and when I'm back, you sure as hell had better be presenting for me like I told you to do!"

I swallowed a whimper, grabbing at his wrist again. My eyes clenched shut, every inch of my body shaking.

"If you fucking disobey me again, I swear to fucking God you'll be sorry." He pushed me to the floor, and I bit back my sobs as he stomped down the hallway.

The front door slammed shut, the roar of Stephen's engine blaring to life then fading as he drove off.

Silence rang in my ears. I clenched my jaw against the wails deep inside me rising to break loose.

Enough, a voice whispered in my head. A lone sob escaped, and I pressed my knuckles to my mouth. *Enough*.

It didn't matter that I had no money of my own. It didn't matter that I would have to head into the unknown to start over. And those twelve years I'd hung my hat on for so damn long sure as hell didn't matter either.

I. Was. Done.

I rolled onto my hands and knees and used the chair I'd

been sitting in to pull myself upright. Zings of pain ran down my legs from where Stephen had kicked me, and I could barely move my left arm.

Another cry ripped from my clenched lips as I staggered toward the entryway.

The liquor store was less than a mile away, which left me all of about five minutes tops to get the hell out of the house.

Rather than going upstairs to grab a bag, I got my purse and coat from the wobbly rack and the car keys off the nail beside the front door. Without a backward glance or taking the time to pull on my coat, I staggered out into the frigid air. My breath fogged with every fast exhale, and I hurried over the icy walkway of uneven bricks the best I could to the cracked driveway.

Fingers fumbling and hysterical half-laughs, half-sobs bursting from my lips, I finally got the old Chevy started and shifted it into reverse.

I backed out onto our street and turned the opposite way Stephen would have gone to the liquor store. My hands clenched the steering wheel in a white-knuckled grip, and I leaned forward to see out of the windshield fogging from my fast exhales.

A flick turned the defrost on, but it failed to work fast enough. I rubbed my forearm on the windshield, desperate to move. *Faster. Take a corner. Another. Speed up. Slow down for the stop sign. Yield into traffic...*

I hit the highway and lay on the gas.

Stephen tried to call, but I ignored my cell, my pulse still thrumming.

Twenty seconds later, the darkened skies opened up, drenching the road and my car. My phone rang again.

The tears fell, deep, guttural whines passed my lips, and

the defrost finally did its thing, the wipers barely able to clear my windshield. I clung to the steering wheel, my left shoulder and lower back on fire.

Twice more, he attempted to call me.

I forced myself to take deep breaths and slow the car down. Calm the hysteria on the cusp of my brain. All I could think about was Chantelle.

I needed my cousin.

Once reasonably sure I had my emotions under control, I fumbled with my phone. I dialed her cell by memory.

She didn't answer, and I hit "end."

The phone rang in my hand. A glance showed Stephen's name. I waited for the ringing to stop, then tried Chantelle again.

More tears slid down my cheeks as my call went to voicemail.

I had been to her condo just the two nights and couldn't for the life of me navigate my way through downtown Boston to find it again. I wasn't about to show up at her kink club, either.

The memory of the scribbled address on the back of Daniel's business card burned in my brain. I had memorized his personal information on the card before throwing it in the trash two hours after he'd given it to me a few weeks earlier.

Any time, he had said.

Brow furrowed and inner lip between my teeth, I ignored Stephen's latest attempt to reach me. Once my cell went silent, I dialed Daniel.

"Hello?" He greeted, his deep voice swept over me, and sobs erupted again, prohibiting me from answering. "Becky?"

"Yes," I somehow managed, slowing down and moving to the far-right lane.

"Are you okay?"

"N-No," I wailed.

"What's wrong? Where are you?" Panic bled through his voice, worsening my misery. He cared. Chantelle hadn't lied. The big, soft giant's emotions surfaced past his seemingly stoic nature for a woman he hardly knew.

My breath caught as intense longing to be near him, to feel his strength, swept through me.

"Stephen?" he asked.

"He's..." I tried to get hold of myself but failed miserably as Stephen himself once more attempted to call me.

"Everything is going to be alright, Becky." Daniel sounded calmer, and I nodded even though he couldn't see me. "Are you driving?"

"Yes," I whispered through my tears.

"Pull over, and I'll come get you."

I inhaled fully, my entire body shuddering from fading adrenaline and a strange mixture of fear and euphoria. "You d-don't have to do that."

"I want to."

"C-can I just stop by your p-place?" The question flew from my lips, every word unstable and rushed. "Chantelle isn't answering her ph-phone, and I d-don't want to be alone." A tremor ripped through me again.

"You know where I live?"

Finding his house wouldn't be a problem, seeing as how I had used Google Maps to locate—memorize—exactly where he lived. I would never admit to being a stalker though. Not even to Chantelle.

"Your card," I reminded him, my tone rasped. Raw. "I'm not too far away...I can drive to your house."

"I'll meet you out front. Just focus on calming your breathing, Becky. You're safe. He can't touch you."

I released a shaky exhale, once more nodding at the truth he spoke. "Be there in about ten minutes." I hit the "end" button and turned off the phone before dropping it onto the passenger seat. The electronic leash deserved to be tossed out the window onto the highway for a date with passing tires, but until I arrived safely at Daniel's, I couldn't chance it.

I pulled into his driveway alongside his SUV.

The sight of his hulking form in the lit garage directly in front of me fluttered my stomach but also sent a strange peace through me.

He motioned me to take my vehicle inside.

Smart, I realized while pulling into the bright interior. If by some stupid chance Stephen figured out where I'd gone, he wouldn't see my car when driving by. I put the Chevy into park, and the garage door slid shut behind me with a loud clanking noise that broke the sudden silence.

Daniel opened my car's squeaky door, and I grabbed my purse, leaving the cell phone on the seat.

He grasped my elbow and helped me out.

I couldn't meet his gaze but stared at the cement floor, my heart pounding, only imagining what he must think of the state of my face.

"Jesus Christ," he bit the words out, causing more tears to well in my eyes. Gentle hands pulled me forward, and I breathed in the scent of citrus and Daniel. I bit the inside of my lip to keep from sobbing again and rested my unbruised cheek on his hard chest.

Hot exhales fanned my forehead, and he kissed my hairline before backing away much too soon. "Let's go inside."

I nodded, and he laced his fingers through mine. My

legs sore and weak, I allowed him to lead me through a door which he locked behind us.

Cherry cabinets, granite countertops, and sparkling stainless-steel appliances met my quick glance around his kitchen.

He sat my purse on the island and lifted my palm to his lips. The softest touch of his mouth on my skin sent a wave of desire through me, but a rush of riotous emotions followed in its wake.

"Can I hold you again, Becky?" His quiet request for consent made my threatening tears even harder to hold back.

I jerked my head yes, and he wrapped his arms around me again in a delicate, calming embrace. Sinking into him was the easiest thing I'd ever done. There was no striving with Daniel, just a simple acceptance, a safe harbor I knew I could trust with my body and emotions.

Large hands soothed up and down my back in a non-sexual way, and I wanted to dive deeper into him, never come up for air.

He was hard all over, a massive, warm giant of a man who could carry the weight of the world on his shoulders without bending.

A shuddering sigh rippled through me in knowing I'd finally made the right choice. That I'd finally put my own safety and mental health first—as I should have done all along.

"Can I get you something to drink?" he murmured against my hair.

"J-just water. Please." I wrapped my arms around my midsection when he released me, realizing as I did so that I had never put on my coat—or replaced the bra I had taken off after getting home from work hours earlier. Not that the latter mattered. Daniel had already seen every inch of my skin anyway.

"Here." He handed me a glass of ice water, and I finally lifted my head.

His brow furrowed as his troubled gaze trailed over the left side of my face.

I raised a hand and ran my fingertips over my swollen cheekbone. "Is it b-bad?"

Lips pursed, he nodded and turned to the freezer. He grabbed a bag of peas and the dish towel hanging by the sink. "Come on." He motioned with his head toward the living room. I made note of a formal dining room off to the right at the front of the house while following him across the sprawling openness of the first floor.

"Sit," he said, his rumbling tone broking no argument but far from unkind.

I lowered myself, trying not to wince from the pain in my back, and he squatted beside my right leg. Eyes full of tenderness and compassion, he gently pressed the dish towel-wrapped peas against my cheek. "Tell me what happened."

Everything that had gone down since that night at Chantelle's poured from my lips. Every humiliating act was disclosed without embarrassment because of the empathy and gentleness Daniel displayed.

His thumb rubbed circles on my kneecap while the other held the ice to my face. A good amount of time passed, but still, I spewed the shit of my life the previous couple of weeks, entrusting him with my emotions.

I swallowed down the last of my ice water and set the empty glass on the coffee table long before I finished.

Daniel laid the peas beside my glass and sat beside me, pulling me against his side as my story wound down. Tears long dried and my voice raspy, I closed my eyes and breathed him in between sentences, loving how his peacefulness seeped into my cells. Unsure of where to put my hands, I rested them in my lap, fingers clasped to keep from grasping him and holding on tight.

"You're staying here tonight," Daniel said once my voice faded. "You can have my room, and I'll sleep on the couch since I haven't gotten around to getting a bed for the spare room yet."

A yawn cracked my jaw as exhaustion settled over my body. "I'll take the couch."

"No, you won't." His firm tone matched the hardness of his chest against my face. He stood and helped me to my feet.

I grimaced while trying to straighten.

"Your back?"

I hummed an affirmative.

"I'll draw a hot bath for you to soak in."

"That actually sounds heavenly," I said, smiling for the first time since I could remember.

A huge bed dominated the far wall of his bedroom, and a massive bathroom sprawled behind the door across from it. The tub was big enough for the both of us with jets, a pampering I'd never experienced before.

He showed me how to turn the jets on and off and retrieved a fluffy gray towel for me before turning to leave.

"Daniel?" I whispered as he reached the bathroom door.

Turning, he lifted his brow. A slew of emotions filled his eyes, ones I didn't have the energy to figure out.

"Thank you." My lips wobbled. "For everything."

He nodded and left me alone, the door giving a soft click as it shut behind him.

I struggled to take off my work shirt and pants but didn't

have the guts to call him back in to help me undress. It took me a little while, but I finally managed to strip and slowly lowered my aching body into the tub.

"Mercy." I groaned at the soothing heat of the water, submerging myself by lying back to rest my head.

He had turned the jets on low, and the gentle pummeling of water against my sore muscles was like the warmest sun on a spring morning. Like his soothing hands. His soft caresses.

Another shuddering sigh rippled through me.

"I'm never going back." My declaration sounded loud in my ears even though I had barely whispered the words. "Never."

Chapter 19

Daniel

I called Chantelle's office and explained what had happened, barely managing to keep my rage contained. While I hadn't seen beneath Becky's clothing, the way she had moved and winced told me bruises littered more than just her cheekbone. "She's staying here with me tonight."

"Hopefully longer," Chantelle murmured.

"Agreed."

"I don't need to tell you to take good care of her, so I won't." Her tone revealed her smile. "Just move slow. Make sure she's ready to move on before you try sleeping with her."

"I think you know me better than that," I said, refilling Becky's glass with ice.

"You're right. Have her call me tomorrow."

"Will do." I hung up and returned to my bedroom, placing the ice water on the bedside table. Hands on hips, I stared at my bed. Becky would be between those sheets like I'd been dreaming about since first meeting her, but she would be there alone.

Inwardly cursing, I grabbed one of the two pillows and a blanket from the linen closet. I'd already pulled on my lounge pants before she had called. Those along with the T-shirt I wore would suffice for sheets.

I tossed my pillow and blanket on the couch, then sat on the cushion's edge and waited. The large clock hanging over the buffet in the dining room clicked loud over the low hum of the bathtub's jets. I could just make out the whirling through both doors closing me off from Becky and her petal-soft skin.

My cock didn't give two shits about the situation that had put her in my home but tented my pants at the thought of her naked. "Goddamnit." I scrubbed my hand down over my face and growled a few more lively curses.

She hadn't lingered to pack a bag which meant she had nothing other than the work clothes she'd had on all day.

I stood and stalked back into the bedroom, my cock leading the way, bouncing with each step. Putting on some tighty-whities would probably be better than commando, I told myself while rifling through my shirts. A soft, worn navy-blue T-shirt would make do for her nightgown. It would also fall close to mid-thigh and tease the shit out of me, but it was all I had.

The jets turned off, and I strained my ears.

A few minutes later, the drain clinked open, and I realized I still stood beside my bureau, shirt in hand. Shaking my head, I made for the bathroom door.

"Becky?"

"I'll be done in a minute."

"I have a T-shirt you can use to sleep in tonight."

The door cracked open. She had wrapped the towel around her torso, the pink, flushed skin of the tops of her water-pebbled breasts calling out to my tongue.

I jerked my attention to her equally flushed face and handed her the shirt.

"Thanks." She smiled, her big brown eyes clearer of the tumultuous emotions from earlier.

"Feeling better?"

Her smile didn't wobble. "A bit."

"Grab your clothes. I'll throw them in the wash."

She put her back toward me, and I enjoyed the sway of her hips as she walked to retrieve them from the vanity. "If you'll show me where the laundry is, I can put them in."

"You relax. I'll take care of it." I accepted the clothing she held out to me.

"Thank you."

I didn't turn away until she shut the door. I acted like a lovestruck teenager and told myself to get a grip.

Her shirt smelled like the coffee shop with a hint of Becky beneath. I dropped the bundle on top of the washer, and a flash of bright pink caught my eye. She'd given me her panties. I pulled them from between her crumpled-up black pants and lifted them to my nose.

My cock sprang back to attention, and I groaned at the musky scent of her pussy clinging to the cotton lining. Drooling like a fucking dog, I sniffed again, filling my lungs with her sweetness.

"Goddamn," I groaned, pressing my heel against the base of my dick.

How the fuck would I sleep knowing she lay in my bed with nothing but my shirt between her and my sheets?

"Fuck." Grumbling, I threw her clothes in the wash and forced my mind onto the big account I hoped to close before the week ended. A nice fat bonus lay in my future if I could make it happen. Once my cock hung semi-limp along my left thigh, I strolled back into the living room.

No Becky.

My bedroom door was still wide open like I'd left it. Becky sat on the edge of the bed, hands in her lap, wet hair hanging around her heart-shaped face.

"Better?" I asked, moving to her side.

"Yes. Thank you." Pink still tinged her cheeks, and she wouldn't look at me.

"I got you more water," I said, motioning toward the glass on the stand she must have already seen, but I didn't know what to say or do. "If you need anything else, just holler."

"Okay," she whispered.

I hesitated a few seconds before turning away. "*Anything...*" I emphasized, hating what my voice hinted at but unable to stop myself. I closed the door behind me without a backward glance.

One heavy exhale, and I cursed my way across the living room.

The couch was no feather bed. The clock ticked, louder and louder as I strained for noises from the bedroom. Tensed body sprawled out, I closed my eyes, forcing myself to count sheep.

Ticktock, one, two... Ticktock, tickety-tock. Ninety-seven, ninety-eight.

I rolled to my side and punched my pillow. It was going to be a long fucking night.

"Daniel?"

I hadn't heard the door open. "Yeah?" I sat up.

Becky stood in my bedroom's threshold, the moonlight pouring in through the living room windows casting her in a half-halo of angelic aura. My gaze latched onto the hem of my T-shirt caressing her upper thighs.

She wrung her hands at her waist, drawing my focus upward.

"Are you okay?" I asked, my voice husky as fuck.

"N-no."

I climbed off the couch and went to her, drawing her into my arms. She smelled like my shampoo, my soap, but the sweet scent of her skin clung beneath, thickening my damn cock. Same as when I'd held her in the kitchen, I kept my hips well back from her body.

Becky trembled in my arms but heaved a heavy breath as I kissed the top of her head. "Would you sleep with me?"

My cock jerked.

"I mean, you make me feel safe, and I...don't want to be alone." The words tumbled from her lips.

"Whatever you need," I said, smoothing my hand down her spine. I would suffer blue balls all night long laying atop the blankets if it meant she would rest peacefully.

I grabbed my pillow and went into the bedroom to find she had already folded down the comforter on my side. Beneath the sheets it would be, then. Jaw clenched, I climbed into the bed beside her curled form. She lay with her back toward me and scooted closer when I didn't touch her.

Not needing a second invite, I curled around her, keeping my raging hard-on from brushing against her lush ass. I laid one arm over the dip of her waist, fist curled to stop myself from running my palm up and over the T-shirt covered breasts I had dreamed of sliding my cock between.

Another clench of my jaw stifled a groan.

"Thank you," she whispered, snuggling against me, bringing the globes of her ass right against my groin. She stilled, her body tensing beneath my curled fingers.

I didn't know if I should apologize or flex my hips so she

could feel what she did to me. I did neither and clenched my eyes shut, focusing on breathing.

Becky didn't pull away but let out a shuddering sigh. "Are you uncomfortable?" she asked, her voice low.

My cock jerked against her ass. "Only in the best way possible," I choked out.

She giggled a little—the first laughter I had ever heard from her.

I opened my eyes and smiled at the dim outline of her head. "Are *you* uncomfortable?"

"Yes."

"In a good way or bad way?" I asked, still smiling.

She wiggled her ass the slightest bit, and I let my groan fly, splaying my fingers across her belly and tightening my arm around her waist. "I'm going to have a very hard time trying to sleep if you keep moving like that."

More light laughter escaped her, but she sobered quickly. "Is it wrong for me to want you at a time like this?"

Goddamnit...the woman was too fucking much.

"No." I rolled Becky onto her back and propped on an elbow to peer down at her. Although darkness hovered over the bedroom, I could easily make out the purple bruise on her cheek. The long, silky lashes framing her wide, doe-like eyes. Her bowed, parted lips needing to be kissed.

I ran my fingertips along her jaw, down to the pulse thrumming in her neck. "Is it wrong that I long to give you whatever you desire right now?" I asked with a similar sentiment, torn between being patient and submitting to the hunger in her eyes.

She stared at my mouth. "No," she echoed my whisper.

Tracing a fingertip over her lips, I swallowed. "Can I kiss you?"

She lifted her head and brushed her lips across mine.

Hand sliding beneath her nape to keep her close, I sank into the sweetest mouth I had ever tasted. Blueberries? Strawberries? Whatever her flavor, I craved more, caressing my tongue along hers. I breathed her exhales deep into my lungs.

With a moan, she relaxed in my hold on her neck, and I lowered her back to the mattress. My mouth still fused to hers, my chest resting half against her softness. I nibbled and licked both of her lips, memorizing every inch of her with my tongue.

A tentative touch on my waist enticed me to shift closer, and she grasped at my T-shirt, holding tight as though afraid I would move away and leave her alone.

I rolled us onto our sides, running my hand along her curves and lifting her leg over my waist. Trailing open-mouthed kisses along her jaw and down her neck, I pressed the back of my leaking cock against her core. The heat of her pussy seared me through my lounge pants, and I ground against her while groaning into her neck.

"Becky," I rasped, too many curses and words of affirmation I wanted to speak but couldn't.

She threaded her fingers through my hair. "Please," she whispered, lifting my head up to kiss her eager lips.

Thrusting my tongue in time with my hips against her core, I slid my hand beneath her ass, filling my palm with her bare, plump flesh. I squeezed and kneaded, and she whimpered in my hold, wiggling. Clinging. Her breaths panted against my lips.

"I-I want you, Daniel. *Please.*"

How the fuck was I supposed to deny the pleading in her voice? I pushed her onto her back and settled between her thighs. One last brush of my lips over hers and I sat on my haunches, ripping off my shirt. She wiggled, pulling my T-shirt up over her head. Her wince made me pause.

"Shoulder hurting?" I asked, running my hand over it while she set my shirt aside with her other hand.

"Yes, but I forget about it when you're kissing me." Her dark eyes bored into me, her chest rising and falling with each quickened breath.

The desire in her stare, the scent of her arousal rising from between her thighs pushed me to the edge, but I hesitated.

"We are moving really fast, Becky. I have no desire to push or rush you into something you might not emotionally be ready for."

She stared up at me, determination in her eyes. "I asked you to come in here to be with me. I initiated this because I need you to show me what intimacy is supposed to be like. Please, Sir."

A shudder ripped through me at the thought of not just our bodies but our spirits intertwining as well. Fuck, did I want that. Desperately.

"Then I will," I promised quietly while running my hands up the insides of her thick thighs. "But I'm not your Sir right now. Just Daniel." My gaze drifting down over her breasts with their hardened points. I dipped my gaze lower, over her soft stomach to the thatch of curls I couldn't wait to bury my face in.

My thumbs swept up along the apex of where her thighs met her labia. Wetness coated the pads of my thumbs, and I trailed them back down as she pressed into my touch with a soft moan, eyelids fluttering shut.

I stilled my hands atop her thighs and waited for her to look at me again, not wanting arousal alone to dictate what happened in the next few moments.

Dark lashes fluttered, and she peered at me with puzzlement etched on her face. "Why did you stop?"

"Becky—if you give yourself to me, I want it all." I warned her, my tone firm. Un-fucking-yielding. "That's the cost of allowing me to love on you. There's no going back."

Her eyebrows smoothed, light and life flaring in her dark eyes. "No going back," she echoed her agreement without hesitation as though sure of my character and the trust she had in me.

I needed absolute consent. "You're *certain* you want to give yourself to me so soon after leaving Stephen?" I hated speaking his name, but Becky and I needed to be on the same path, our thoughts and desires aligned in order move forward together.

"Yes."

Thank fucking Christ.

I stroked through her slickness with a single fingertip, and she gasped, lifting her hips. "Show me, Daniel."

I groaned at my name on her lips before stretching out and tucking in to feast on her sweetness.

Chapter 20

Becky

"**O**h. My. God." I shuddered as Daniel licked up through my folds, a deep groan rumbling from his chest. My core pulsed to be filled, and I writhed against his mouth as he continued to lap at my wetness.

Never...it had *never* been this good.

All thoughts of my past fled as he pressed two fingers deep inside me, my slick channel easing his way.

Yes, I hissed the word in my head while grabbing hold of his hair.

He rumbled his appreciation of my taste again, flicking his tongue over where he fucked his fingers into me. "So sweet," he murmured against my labia. "Knew you would be." Daniel moaned, sucking on my flesh, nipping with sharp teeth, the slight sting only intensifying my arousal.

His fingers made lewd, sloppy noises while fucking into me.

"More," I gasped, lifting my hips and tugging his head toward the aching nub amidst my curls.

"Mmm," he hummed and flicked his tongue over my clit while pressing a third finger into my pussy.

Curses spilled from my lips as I clenched my thighs tight against my hands holding his head in place. "Daniel..."

He wrapped his lips around my clit and suckled, his fingers deep inside me, stroking...building a fire inside my core until I panted for breath with little whines building in my chest.

My toes tingled, heart pounded in my ears.

Shivers slid upward from my tailbone to my nape, arching my back.

"Y-You're going to make me come—" I detonated, a shriek flying past my lips. Intense pulses rippled through my pussy, pulling grunts from my lungs. Tremors shook the rest of my muscles, spasming my entire body.

Mind and soul soaring, I drowned in the sensation, wishing I could linger in the sense of euphoria forever.

Daniel groaned and lapped at the wetness leaking from me.

I jolted one last time and sagged on his bed, my breaths still heavy. "Oh, God." I gulped, one last full-body twitch shifting my weight.

"So goddamn sweet," he murmured against my pussy, easing his fingers from me.

I whimpered at the sense of emptiness, wishing he could stay inside me forever. Sudden tears stung my eyes, and I reached for him. "I-I need..."

Daniel sat and leaned over, grabbing a condom from his bedside table.

I lifted onto my elbows and watched as he rolled the rubber down over his thickness. My dry mouth suddenly flooded with drool. I'd always hated to get on my knees but in that moment? I wanted the heaviness of Daniel's cock on my tongue. Lusted to taste his bitter saltiness in my mouth. I longed to swallow him down until he lay spent and sprawled out in bliss like I'd been seconds earlier.

Heat swept over me as I eyed his massive length.

"I-I don't think you're going to fit," I whispered even though I had every intention of finding out.

"Oh, I'll fit," Daniel assured me with a smirk while sliding his finger into my body again. His cock jerked at my needy whimper as he rubbed deep inside my inner wall. "You're soaked for me."

I closed my eyes and ground against his palm fit tight against my core. "Yes," I gasped as he slid his finger out.

Daniel shifted forward, wrapped his hands around my splayed thighs, and pressed the tip of his cock against my entrance. "Look at me while I make you mine, Becky."

I fluttered my eyelids open, my breath catching at the heat, the desire, in Daniel's steady gaze. No one, not even Stephen, had ever looked at me as Daniel did—like I hung the stars in the inky expanse of the night sky. His face appeared as though I had shifted clouds to allow sunlight to filter onto his cold face.

My breath caught, and I swallowed hard, reaching for his wrists to center myself—feel that the moment was real, that *Daniel* was real.

He pressed forward without hindrance, the slow feeling of fullness more intense than anything I'd experienced. It was an invasion of more than flesh and blood. His soul seemed to sink into mine, slow and sure, taking up residence inside my body.

"O-oh..." I bit my lip as he sank deeper. "G-God." A shudder rippled through me as Daniel's groin pressed tight against me. We were a perfect fit.

I'd never felt so filled—*complete.*

Tears stung my eyes even as I continued to keep them on his dark ones.

Leaning forward, Daniel propped on an elbow beside my shoulder, his other hand gripping my thigh. Our gazes remained locked, the stillness like a hovering storm heightening my heartbeat.

"There's no going back," he reminded me while flexing his hips and burrowing incredibly deeper.

"N-never," I vowed on a gasp, recognizing in our coming together that Daniel had been meant for me from the very beginning. Nothing existed but him, and my past no longer mattered.

He leaned in to kiss me, unhurried and relaxed while pulling out until only the head of his cock remained clamped by my pussy. "You're mine," he whispered against my lips and slid in until his pubic bone ground against my clit.

My back bowed, and I cried out against his mouth as another wave of electrical pulses clamped my core around his girth.

He held steady with slow strokes, drawing out my second climax until I shivered beneath his heat, my breath catching.

Nuzzling his lips beneath my ear, he groaned as though fighting for control.

"A-are you okay?" I whispered and could feel his resulting smile against the skin of my neck where his clipped beard tickled.

"Better than okay." He grasped my thigh, nudging against my cervix, and I gasped again. "Wrap your legs around me, sweetness."

I did as told, grabbing hold of his wide shoulders as well.

Daniel angled his hips and shoved forward. Hard.

"Oh, God!" My legs squeezed, hands grasping at his hard muscles. "M-More. Please," I begged, uncaring that I sounded like a needy whore.

He set a steady pace, thrusting and grinding against my core. "I knew you would feel like heaven," he growled and planked over me, glancing down to where our bodies joined.

I leaned up to do the same, my mouth going dry at the sight of his length spearing into me, wetness glistening around his thickness. My pussy welcomed him with an eagerness I hadn't expected. Everything inside me tingled at the heat of him—how he stuffed me full with every inch of his cock.

"Daniel," I whispered his name, my voice catching at the rush of arousal sweeping over me.

He once more leaned down and captured my mouth with a groan. Hips upping their pace, he rocked into me. "So fucking good..."

I moaned, lifting to meet his every thrust.

"I want you to come around my cock again." He nipped my lower lip. "Tighten that hot pussy around me and milk me dry."

His words swirled lust through my blood, and I yearned to give him what he asked for. Hands grasping at his tensed shoulders, I closed my eyes and gave over the sensations surrounding me as he ate at my mouth. Heat. Slickness between my thighs and along his tongue. The hardness filling me. A delicious aching in my chest...stinging in my eyes.

I pulled my mouth from his, gasping for breath. "Daniel," I whispered again. "Please..."

He hissed and slammed into me, my back arching, my breasts pressing against his chest. "My sweet Becky." A guttural grunt fled his lips as he bucked harshly against my cervix.

A third climax swept through me, and I bit my lower lip, a low moan escaping me.

"Jesus...fuck." Daniel's cock bucked inside me, throbbing as he came. He groaned against my neck. Nipped my jaw. Licked at my mouth.

We shared gasped breaths, drinking in the other's soft noises from having found release while wrapped up inside one another.

Our inhales slowed, heartbeats calmed, and our kisses turned languid as he stilled inside me. He brushed his lips over the skin beneath my ear, and I angled my head to give him better access.

A shuddering sigh rippled through my body. I wanted to soak in the heat of him clear through my soul he'd attached himself to. Keep his thickness stuffed all up in my core for eternity.

"You okay?" he murmured against my ear, sending a shiver over my skin.

"Mmm." Had his weight not pressed gloriously atop me, I would have stretched like a lazy cat.

With a groan, he lifted onto his elbows.

Sated, dark eyes peered down at me in the dim light, and I couldn't contain my smile from the well of happiness bubbling up inside me.

He cradled my jaw in his large hands, thumbs rubbing over my lips. "You are so goddamn beautiful, Becky."

Joy swept through me even as peace stole in to keep my mind clear, my body relaxed beneath him. "Thank you," I whispered, unable to put into words how much I appreciated the man on me—*in* me.

"Stay here." He kissed me softly, the tenderness of his

palms on my face sending affection for him rushing through my heart. "I'll get a washcloth and clean you up."

I winced as he pulled away, a chill sweeping over my skin at the loss of his heat.

But I sighed in complete and utter bliss, the sense of finding my home making gratitude swell in my chest.

Chapter 21

Daniel

My heart full and dick thoroughly satisfied, I took care of business with a goofy-ass grin. A glance in the mirror while wetting a washcloth revealed a flushed face and sated eyes peering back at me.

Becky had come to me in her time of need.

Me. Not Chantelle, her cousin, but a man she barely knew. It revealed her trust, her sense of feeling safe with me, that rightness I'd experienced the first time I'd brushed my fingertips against her skin all those weeks ago.

A well of...*something* rose inside my chest, achy and addictive. She had given herself to me willingly. Begged for me to pleasure her in a way only I had ever accomplished.

Talk about a fucking ego boost atop soul-deep satisfaction from claiming the only woman I'd ever wanted burrowed deep inside my heart.

Still smirking, I left the bathroom light on so I could better see Becky and returned to my bedroom with the towel to clean her up.

Her eyes followed my every step, her focus flitting down over my body, appreciation in her gaze.

She had taken all of me. Hadn't shied away from the girth of my dick or how I dwarfed her size with my mass. Becky Eaton was damn perfect for me in every way.

She reached for the washcloth, but I shook my head and settled between her thighs again. Pink flushed her from head to toe, and I imagined the marks my ropes had indented into her skin what seemed ages ago, the flesh plumping between wraps I hadn't gotten to thoroughly squeeze and caress.

Someday soon, I promised myself.

I wiped her cum from between her thighs, and she shifted and sighed, her long eyelashes closing in rest.

I tossed the towel to the bedside table and stared down at the swollen, reddened lips of her labia and the nub surrounded by black curls. "You're perfect," I said, sweeping my thumb over her pubic bone.

She smiled, her eyes warm and restful. Her gaze summoned me, and I stretched out beside her, rolling her a bit so we faced each other, my leg snaked between hers. Becky winced.

"Okay?"

"Ribs hurt a little bit."

Jaw clenched, I tucked some dark hair behind her ear, taking in the light spattering of freckles over the bridge of her nose. The purple on her cheekbone.

I feathered my fingertips over the bruise. "Does this ache too?"

"No."

"I can get some ice—"

"No." She clutched at my shoulder to keep me close, her soft breasts pressing against my chest.

We shared exhales, her breath smelling sweet as strawberries. Our eyes latched together as quietness settled between us. No discomfort or strangeness rose to soil the air, simply a peaceful existence at that moment. Enjoying the tingles through extremities of having found release.

"I meant what I said," I murmured, studying her eyes for any indication she felt differently after having experienced intimacy for the first time. "There's no going back, Becky."

Her smile sent happiness radiating through my chest, a pure and unhindered response to my words. "Good luck getting rid of me."

I snorted. "As if I would ever want to."

Her lips slowly relaxed, seriousness lining her face. "This doesn't seem real—how I feel about you. I don't *know* you. We have no shared history, no foundation to explain my emotions toward you."

"I'm calling bullshit." I gently tugged her closer, running my fingertips over her spine. "We don't have a lot of past experiences together, but we're going to remedy that. There's a draw between us, something potent as fuck, and whether we spend one hour or fifty together, I'm sure that you were put on this earth to walk beside me."

Wetness welled in her eyes.

"You can't deny your soul calls out to mine, sweetness. I could feel it while buried deep inside you."

"Same," she whispered, solidifying my claim inside my heart and mind.

"I will never leash or lead you around like a sex slave," I promised. "There will never be any demands on my lips that aren't meant to bring you pleasure. You hold the power, Becky. You'll *always* be the one in control."

I swiped an escaped tear off her bruised skin, pushing against the darkness wanting to rile up inside me.

"Can I tell you a story?" I asked, my voice low even though a trace of adrenaline leaked into my bloodstream.

She nodded, her hand still holding tight to my shoulder.

I inhaled fully and slowly emptied my lungs. "My father was abusive to my mom."

Becky swallowed, and another tear leaked from eyes full of empathy and understanding.

"When I was old enough to understand what was happening, Mom hid me in a kitchen cabinet if he came home on a rampage. As I grew older, she begged me to look the other way. Run and hide so he would exercise his demons on her alone.

"Regardless of how he hurt her, she remained faithful as far as I knew. She cooked and cleaned, took care of me and his household since he worked outside the home to provide for us. I was thirteen when Mom finally admitted to herself who—*what*—he was. She told me to pack a bag, but he came home early and caught us leaving."

Becky placed her palm on my cheek, her touch warm and grounding.

Thickness grew in my throat as another droplet of wetness slid from her eye.

"Did he hurt you too?" she whispered.

I shook my head. "Never. That afternoon—" I cleared my throat, trying to steady my voice. "One punch dropped her to her knees, then he dragged her back into the house while I stood frozen in the front yard. Anger rose to choke out my fear, and I went inside. Mom's whimpers drew me toward the kitchen. He had tied her to a chair."

"Daniel..." Becky's voice broke, and I closed my eyes.

"He punched her again with enough force to snap her neck."

"Oh, God."

"He'd gone too far in his anger—and he knew it within seconds. Unfortunately, that time, his pleading for forgiveness, his begging her to stay with him didn't work. She didn't respond. *Couldn't*."

The memory, the nightmare that visited me some nights, flashed through my head, and same as always, I couldn't remember what had prompted my actions. I'd said instinct when interrogated by the police. I'd claimed it had been a need to protect even though she'd already been gone when I'd moved across the kitchen.

"I picked up the cast-iron skillet off the stovetop," I told Becky what no one else in my adult life knew. "Kneeling in front of my mom's corpse, screaming, my father didn't hear me come up behind him. He deserved to suffer tenfold what he'd rained down on my mom, but I just wanted him gone. He took my mom from me—so I exacted vengeance without remorse."

I opened my eyes, expecting to see judgment. Horror at the very least.

The softness in Becky's gaze remained. She didn't suggest I'd done the right thing, didn't say he deserved what he got.

She fucking knew firsthand.

"What I feel for you," I stated slowly, studying every line of her face, "is more than an instinct to keep you safe, Becky. I don't want you to think that I'm drawn to you simply because of my past. Everything about you calls out to me—entices me to snake closer. Touch and taste. Share your breaths and listen to your voice. I long to drown myself in your sweetness and never come up for air. Ever—if you'll let me."

More tears slid down her cheeks, and I tucked her in close against my neck, her warm exhales ghosting over my skin.

I'd fallen hard for Becky, and nothing would keep me from providing for her. Loving her.

Protecting her.

Chapter 22

Becky

I drifted off to a dreamless, easy sleep after hours of talking with Daniel, my mind quiet and peaceful for the first time in years. When consciousness returned, I found myself still wrapped in strong arms, cocooned in warmth and safety.

A sigh shuddered through me, and I turned to rub my face against Daniel's hard chest. Soft skin over steel...like the length of him digging into my thigh.

I pulled my head back a bit.

Sleepy dark eyes, long reddish eyelashes, and a killer smirk greeted my bleary eyes.

"Morning," his deep voice rumbled, pebbling my skin with goose bumps.

My nipples ached for attention, and heat settled between my thighs. "Morning." I had never appreciated the thought or feel of a morning erection before, but Daniel's hardness pressing against me had all sorts of naughtiness flooding my mind.

On a whim, I reached my hand between us and wrapped my hand around him.

He groaned and closed his eyes, shifting his hips back to give me room to play. Pre-cum smeared along my palm as I rubbed over the head of his thick length.

Mouth watering, I slid downward, intent on coating my tongue with his flavor. The thought of his cock filling my mouth sent a rush of wetness to coat my thighs. I couldn't get down there fast enough.

"You don't have to do that, Becky," he said but didn't try to stop me.

"I've never actually desired to do this before, but with you?" I shoved at the sheets to bare him in the morning light. Flushed and veined, his cock beckoned like the sweetest lollipop.

I closed my mouth over him, the slightly bitter tang of his pre-cum hitting my taste buds. "Mmm," I hummed, taking him as deep as I could go. My gag reflex kicked in, making my eyes water.

"Oh, fuck," he growled, his hands grasping the sides of my head as I slid down over his length once more. "God, Becky."

He allowed me control, simply cradling my head in his huge hands as I swirled my tongue around and down, hollowing my cheeks and sucking every drop of pre-cum I could entice from his drawn-up balls.

My vaginal walls clenched and released on their own, and I pressed my thighs together, a maddening need for him spurring me on. The head of his cock rubbed against the back of my throat, but I exhaled through my nose and relaxed so I wouldn't gag again.

Daniel thrust gently once—twice—before I lifted up and swiped my tongue over the weeping head of him. A soft graze of my teeth, and I sank to swallow around him, tugging on his balls with my hand.

"I want you, God, how I want you." He grabbed hold of my uninjured arm, pulling me off his cock and up over his body.

I went willingly, only a brief thought of my weight atop him before he captured my lips and obliterated all thought. He groaned into my mouth and rubbed the back of his length up through my soaked folds.

He rolled us and slid deep into my pussy with one slow thrust, swallowing my gasp at the quick but painlessly full feeling.

"Shit...condom." He stilled inside of me, the muscles of his back tense beneath my hands.

"I'm on the pill and negative," I whispered against his ear. "Don't stop. Please—unless you need to."

He groaned my name, slid out, and pressed in deep again. "I'm negative too." His ass flexed beneath my heels. "You feel so fucking good. I'll never get enough of you."

The friction between our bodies created more moisture inside me, slickening and heightening my arousal. I panted for breath, my heartbeat pounding in my ears. I spiraled toward release and wanted Daniel to come inside of me.

But, I wasn't ready for the sweet moment to end.

Daniel gathered one of my breasts in his hands and suckled my tight nipple into his mouth. A shot of lightning zinged straight to my clit, and I gasped, arching my back.

"Like that?" he asked and sucked harder.

"Oh, yes—"

His teeth scraped over the sensitive flesh, and I squeezed my inner walls around him as he slid out.

"One day, I'm going to fuck these gorgeous, huge tits." He thumbed over my sensitive nipple, and I moaned, writhing with need and emotion I couldn't begin to comprehend.

I hitched one leg around his waist and held on tight as he angled, deepening his thrusts.

He released his hold on my breast and reached between us, sliding a fingertip down over my throbbing clit. "I want you to come for me, Becky," he whispered, lowering his head. His lips brushed across mine. "Want your cum soaking my cock and dripping on my bed. Want to hear you cry out my name." He tugged on my bundle of nerves, enticing my body to give him what he craved.

Tingles lit in my toes and swept up my legs into my center. My climax rolled over me, and I fulfilled his requests, grasping at him until he growled his own release and buried his face in my neck.

JF

I ran my fingertips over the dip and swell of Daniel's chest. The slightest bit of auburn hair was soft to the touch and his pebbled nipples...I pinched one.

He groaned, grabbed my hand, and brought it to his lips.

I snuggled against him. "I finally understand what it means to be insatiable," I murmured, losing myself to his tongue flicking over and around my fingers.

"Mmm."

"But—" I pulled back and smiled "—we both have to work."

"I think you should take a sick day," Daniel said, brushing my hair off of my forehead with a gentle touch. "I don't trust Stephen."

"I don't either, but he's never shown up at the coffee shop no matter how upset he's been with me."

"Have you ever tried leaving him before?"

"Well, except for those two nights at Chantelle's, no."

Daniel raised an eyebrow, and I considered his question while chewing on the inside of my lip.

"I would sit outside the coffee shop all day if I could to keep an eye on you, but I've got a huge meeting today at noon."

Lightness floated in my chest, and I smiled again. "You're a good man, Daniel Cooney," I said, leaning forward to press my lips against his. He might have murdered his father, but in the moment I had declared to myself that I'd had enough of Stephen's abuse, I would have hit him over the head with a skillet too, given the chance. That understanding, the shared history between us only deepened the connection I felt with him.

Daniel's actions, whether considered before moving to his mother's stove or not, had been an act of desperation, an instinct to survive. Nothing about Daniel made me consider him to be a violent man. He'd done what was needed as far as I was concerned. An eye for an eye.

While I really didn't wish Stephen dead, I also wanted nothing to do with him. Whatever softness I'd had in my heart, whatever pitying empathy that had caused me to stay as long as I had beneath his abuse, had dissipated. Those feelings no longer existed. They had been wiped clean by a change of mind, a decision long in coming. And the gentle touch of a Dom determined to bring me only pleasure solidified my intentions to continue pressing forward in my new life.

Would it include Daniel? His claims suggested it would, and I hoped so.

Time would tell.

Losing myself in his kisses was easy. Submitting myself to him came naturally—but I also recognized I needed to be me. *Find* me—the new Becky Eaton who took charge of her life and stood on her own without influence.

I pulled back from Daniel's mouth and heaved a sighed exhale. We both had responsibilities to take care of, and I planned on facing mine that day with a real smile on my face for a change. I'd finally chosen right, but there would be a need for honesty with my friends and family in order for me to remain safe.

"I'll tell my boss what happened and have him call the police if Stephen shows up and causes problems," I murmured, feathering my fingertip over Daniel's lower lip.

"Promise?" The worry in his gaze flooded my heart with warmth.

"Yes."

"Call me if you need me." His voice didn't hint at suggestion, but those words were an order I wouldn't mind obeying in the least.

"I will."

He kissed my fingertip. "When do you have to go in?" he asked, rubbing the back of my hand down his bristly jaw.

"Ten. What time is it now?"

He craned his neck to look over his shoulder at the alarm clock on the bedside table. "Nine."

"I need to get moving," I said, but I didn't budge. "Thank you." I gazed into his dark chocolate-like eyes, butterflies taking to flight in my stomach. "For everything."

"There's nothing I wouldn't give to keep you safe—and thank *you* for allowing me to love on your beautiful body."

Warmth flushed through me.

"You're coming back here after work," he said, snuggling down lower against me, burying his face in my neck, his scruff tickling me.

"Yes."

"And we'll talk about getting your belongings out of Stephen's house tonight."

I sobered real quick at the thought of that necessary showdown. Having Daniel at my side would make things a million times easier. "Okay."

With a groan, Daniel rolled away from me and climbed off the bed.

My gaze was glued to his ass as he walked across the room, every step flexing his muscular cheeks.

"Thought you needed to get going," he said with a chuckle, bending to grab a pair of jeans from a drawer.

"Yeah." I scooted off his bed and grabbed the T-shirt he'd given me the night before. "Did you happen to throw my clothes in the dryer, or am I going to be late?" I asked, pulling it over my head.

"I snuck out to do it after you fell asleep last night. You are so beautiful."

I caught his stare and blushed. Never had a man been so liberal with his compliments. If not for the lust in his eyes and the fact he'd already had me in his bed, I would have sworn he lied.

A tumult of emotions rolled over me, thickening my throat. "You're the sexiest, sweetest man I've ever met," I whispered and hurried to the bathroom before he saw the moisture gathering in my eyes.

With the rising of the sun and physical distance from Daniel, reality and a slew of thoughts slammed into my brain. I grabbed hold of the sink to keep myself upright. Stephen would be livid I hadn't been home when he'd returned from the liquor store. Had he drunk himself into a stupor? Driven around searching for me? Called the cops?

I chewed the inside of my lip, thinking about work. *Would* he show up at the coffee shop and cause problems?

Closing my eyes, I drew a deep breath, trying to calm my heightened pulse. I would focus on serving customers, hurry back to Daniel, then deal with the Stephen situation with my Sir's help. Maybe even the police.

God knew I wouldn't have the strength to handle it on my own, no matter how much I wanted to.

"Cream and sugar in your coffee, right?" Daniel called through the bathroom door.

The tension in my stomach eased as a smile lifted my lips again. "Yes, please."

"I'll go get your clothes," he said. "There's a new toothbrush in the top drawer."

"Thank you." I peered at myself in the mirror. With no makeup on hand, the bruise on my cheek would draw all kinds of attention.

A day earlier, I would have said that I'd tripped and fallen. I lifted my chin, preparing myself for the truth.

"My ex smashed my face against the table," I murmured what I intended to tell everyone who asked.

It served Stephen right to be exposed for what he was, what Chantelle had been trying to tell me for years. Doing so would shame me as well. I had stayed too long and wasted some of the best years of my life.

Torn on what to think about *that* fact, I studied my face. My eyes were shit brown and boring but sparkled like I had never seen. Pink flushed my cheeks, and my lips were reddened and puffed from kissing. Daniel's scruff had marked up my neck, but I expected it would fade before I got to work.

I looked like a woman who had been loved on all night long, and I felt...beautiful, just as Daniel had claimed.

"Clothes are on the bed." His bass voice rumbled

through the door again, sending a needy twinge between my thighs.

My face heated. I was insatiable for him and would rather stay in bed all day long than toast bagels and pour coffee for five hours.

"Chantelle called me looking for you—said she'd returned your call last night and that you still weren't answering this morning. I hope it's okay that I told her you were here."

"That's fine—thank you. I'll get in touch with her over my break."

A few minutes later, I joined him in the kitchen where he handed me a travel mug of coffee.

"I'll be home around six," Daniel whispered into my hair while squeezing me tight. "But call me if you need me."

"I will."

One last brush of our lips, and I hurried out the kitchen door and into my clunker that Daniel had heated up for me.

My cell sat on the passenger seat, still turned off.

I powered it up, not surprised to find dozens of notifications. Stephen had been relentless as I expected, but I only cared that my cousin had rung me back the night before. She'd also left three messages that morning.

I quickly texted back, letting her know that I would call her over my break to fill her in on what had happened.

Daniel still stood in the driveway, shoulders hunched against the cold as I backed onto the street. I fluttered my fingers, smiling, as he waved.

I'd had a taste of what a good relationship could and should be like, and I had zero desire to go back to what had been before. Excitement for the day to end so I could return to Daniel kept my blood pumping. I'd never felt so...high before. A natural excitement that made everything about the cold April morning burst with color. Budding green leaves, cobalt blue sky, and yellow daffodils greeted my gaze every time I glanced away from the road.

I ended up being ten minutes late for work and took an additional five to quickly explain to my boss what had happened with Stephen the evening before. He promised to be on the lookout for my ex, and I went behind the counter.

My bruise drew a lot of empathetic attention, and I went with the truth as I'd decided. Yes, I had been a moron for having stayed as long as I did, but I was proud of my decision to leave him. So were my co-workers.

The morning sped by, and I smiled, making eye contact with customers rather than staying to myself and watching the floor between filling orders. Encouraging smiles and kind words compounded the peace I experienced over my new beginning. I hardly thought of Stephen.

Until break.

He came in for coffee, eyes red, but from booze or tears, I couldn't tell. Lines and bags under his eyes made him appear older than his twenty-nine years. He looked like a pathetic, beaten dog. Not one ounce of pity or empathy flooded me like it would have done a day ago.

My stomach clenched, and my heart sped as he neared the counter, and once he moved my way, I turned toward him.

"Can we talk?" he asked, his voice breaking.

I glanced around. My boss watched from the register, and I smiled to ease his frown even though the last thing I felt was happy.

Holding my shoulders back and my head up, I gave Stephen my attention. I was done cowering under his gaze. Done submitting to the abusive authority I had given him for so long. "I go on break in a few minutes," I said, my voice even and firm.

He swallowed and nodded, but I remained unmoved by his apologetic puppy dog eyes I'd fallen for a hundred times too many. "I'll wait in my car." He shuffled out the door and toward the right, out of view.

My breath left in a rush and I sagged, shaky from the adrenaline crash.

"Everything okay?" my boss asked as I entered the back room a minute later.

"Yes. He's in his apologetic stage of this shitty game I am so over." I huffed a snort of unfunny laughter that shook along with my voice. "He'll grovel and beg for another chance, but this time he's out of luck."

"I'm not sure talking to him is a good idea."

"I'll be fine. He won't hurt me if others are around. He has a high opinion of himself and he'll do anything to uphold it."

My boss huffed. "Just stay close to the windows. I'll be out in a minute to keep an eye on you."

"I will, thanks." I grabbed my coat and headed out the front door.

Stephen's car sat two spaces to the right, and he rolled down his window as I drew near, clutching my coat close against the cold. "Hop in," he said, pulling papers and a sweatshirt off of the passenger seat.

"I'm good," I said, not moving.

"Please, Becky. I just want to talk, and there's no sense in you standing out in the cold."

The winter wind bit my cheeks, and I admitted to myself he had a point. I nodded and rounded the car, climbing in since customers were coming and going.

Stephen wouldn't dare touch me in public.

The interior stank of stale beer and body odor. Even though my insides shivered and my pulse stuttered, I inhaled shallow breaths. I had decided to keep things short and to the point, no arguing. "I'm moving out, Stephen," I said, angling to face him.

His gaze narrowed, all trace of remorse gone from his eyes. "The fuck you are."

His fist shot out, and I didn't have time to wince. Pain exploded across the bruise on my cheek, and my head crashed into the passenger window. Black spots ate up my vision, devouring my consciousness.

Chapter 23

Daniel

My meeting ran long, and I had a hell of a time focusing on what I needed to be saying and doing to close the biggest deal of my communications business life. A six-figure bonus awaited me if I managed it properly.

It was four o'clock before I left Hartford, and by the time I drove down my street, darkness lay like a thick blanket over the sky. Becky hadn't called or texted, but I wasn't concerned since I hadn't asked her to.

A few minutes from my exit, my cell lit up.

Chantelle.

"Is Becky with you?" she asked instead of greeting me when I answered.

"No—why?"

"She was supposed to call me and never did. I had issues at the club this afternoon and got caught up in a bunch of legal shit. Anyway, I just realized I hadn't heard from her, and now she's not answering."

"Maybe she's in the shower."

"I don't have a good feeling, Daniel."

Neither did I.

I raced into my neighborhood. No light shone from my house windows, and my gut twisted, instant wariness making my arm hair stand on end. I hit the button for the garage door.

Empty.

"Fuck." I parked in the driveway and yanked off my tie. "She isn't here."

"Jesus fucking Christ," Chantelle hissed. "I swear on all things holy I don't even believe in that if that fucker somehow got his claws into her again, I'll skin him alive!"

"I'm going to get in touch with her boss," I said, shifting my SUV back into reverse. "I'll let you know once I learn what the fuck is going on."

I put through a call to the coffee shop to learn the owner had left for the day. Begging and explaining the situation earned me his cell number. I tore back toward the highway the second her boss told me what had happened.

Stephen had shown up, and Becky had gone outside to speak with him over her break. She never returned. Her car remained parked behind their building. Her boss didn't know about me or Chantelle. He'd contacted the police, but until she'd been missing for twenty-four hours, they wouldn't do more than a drive-by of Becky and Stephen's house. The police had reported back to her boss that the house appeared empty with no cars in the driveway.

Dread curled in my stomach, and I raced up the highway, granny drivers and assholes unaware of the insults and curses I spewed their way. I barked out to Siri to text Chantelle letting her know I was headed to Stephen's house.

She called and said she would meet me there, but I told her to stay at the club in case Becky came looking for her.

The rage I kept on a tight leash simmered beneath the surface of my skin, making me hot. Sweaty. I cracked the windows while barreling down the exit, the cool evening air refreshing and invigorating. My muscles all lay in wait, tense and ready on a short fuse.

I slowed to a crawl at the end of Stephen's street. No lights shone from the interior that I could see, but with some of the windows boarded up, that didn't mean shit.

No car sat in the driveway or in front of the house, exactly as the police had claimed.

I stopped alongside the neighbor's and killed the engine, gaze glued to the ramshackle pile of shit Becky had been living in, a million plans racing through my head. Call the police again—and tell them what? Domestic violence had perhaps taken place, but there was no evidence from the dark, still house. Should I sneak in and possibly get shot or arrested for breaking and entering?

Concern for Becky decided for me.

"Fuck it." I grabbed my five-inch blade out of the glove compartment and shoved it into my pocket.

I stalked up to the front door without a coat, my breath in puffs of white leading the way. I banged on the old wooden door, shaking it on its hinges. I counted to ten.

No one answered.

I thumped again, my gut telling me I needed to get inside. A quick study of both windows didn't reveal a damned thing except darkness coating the room beyond. I strode around the north side of the house through overgrown dead weeds from the summer before, kicking down the rickety gate to a half-toppled fence leading into the tiny backyard.

The back stoop was worse off than the front, with more broken pieces of cement than not. With a lack of street light, darkness hovered like a black cloak. I tried the door handle and found it locked.

"Fuck this." I fished out my knife and kicked at the door, uncaring of the dress shoes I wore. The door cracked by the lock, and I kicked again.

It swung open.

"Becky!" I hollered, entering into the dark kitchen.

A muffled yell came from my left.

Without giving heed to danger, I sprinted a few steps and threw the door open. Stairs led downward into the basement. "Becky!" I raced down, stumbling to a stop as I took in the dungeon-like room. A dozen or so candles burned around the musty space, but all I saw was Becky.

Ball-gagged and tied spread eagle to a cross, cane welts and open wounds covering her chest, stomach, and thighs.

White-hot anger lit inside my guts, but I swallowed it, needing to keep my cool. A quick sweep of the room let me know Stephen wasn't with us.

I hurried to Becky's side. "Shh..." I murmured as she stared up at me with wide, terror-filled eyes, tears dripping from her chin. Her nose ran, mixing with the saliva oozing from around the black ball Stephen had shoved into her mouth. Breath panting through her widened nostrils, she moaned.

"Shh..." I whispered, pulling off the gag from around her head.

She sobbed, and the sound tore at my heart.

"I'm getting you out of here," I said, using my knife to cut the cruel synthetic ropes from her ankles.

She shivered and continued to cry, more like a mewing whine, and fell into me the second I freed her wrists. Goose bumps covered her cool skin, and I became aware of the freezing temperature of the room as I wrapped my arms around her, keeping her upright.

"Christ."

A blanket lay askew on the sheet-free mattress tucked against a corner of the basement.

Swinging Becky up into my arms, I set my sights on getting her across the open area and wrapped up tight.

I put her down on the mattress's edge and draped the blanket over her shoulders. "Can you stand up, sweetness?" I murmured, tucking hair away from her face.

Eyes closed, she jerked her head in a nod but struggled to carry any weight while once more leaning against me.

Cradled to my side, she shuffled forward as I led us toward the stairs. No fucking way would she be able to climb them.

Once more, I hefted her into my arms, and she let out a gasp that had me clenching my jaw tight.

"T-too heavy," she murmured but didn't argue any further.

My gaze flitted around the kitchen when I reached the top stair, and I strained my ears for any noise. We still seemed to be alone.

I managed to flip the lock on the front door without putting her down. The driveway and street sat empty.

A few quick strides took me to my SUV. I didn't feel the cold, but Becky seemed to, shivering to the point I struggled to keep hold of her.

Shock, I realized once I stood beside my back door.

"I'm sorry, sweetness, but you have to stand for two seconds so I can open the car door." I slid Becky to her feet, cursing myself for not thinking ahead, but I'd been so focused on getting her out of the damn house that clothing, let alone socks and shoes, hadn't crossed my mind.

I yanked open the door and helped her crawl in, tucking the blanket around her as she curled into a fetal position on my back seat.

"Do you need me to get anything from the house?"

"N-nothing." A shudder rippled the blanket around her. "He already s-smashed or ripped up all my personal items. C-Clothes t-too." Her hoarse voice escaped from the confines of her covering, and I clenched my jaw as a sob followed her words.

I wanted to kill the motherfucker. Tear off his arms and legs and burn his body until nothing but ash and bone remained.

Body tensed, rage screaming for release, I climbed into the car and started the engine. My jaw ached, my stomach a goddamned rock. I flicked the heat on full blast even though sweat soaked my button-down.

Lawrence General was less than ten minutes away, but I hopped back onto the highway, heading south to Melrose-Wakefield.

"You're going to be okay," I swore, the sniffling from the back seat driving me to the point of madness. "I'll never let him near you again. Ever."

"Th-thank you for rescuing m-me," Becky whispered.

"I should have come sooner. I'm so sorry. So fucking sorry." I pounded a fist on my steering wheel, my insides twisting hard enough my abs clenched. "I should have known better. Shouldn't have let you go to work this morning."

"N-Not your fault," she murmured, her scratchy voice fading.

A thought near choked off my breath. "Did he give you anything? Drugs? Anything to drink?"

"N-no, and I'm s-so thirsty."

Teeth clenched, I broke every law making my way to the hospital.

I parked in front of the ER entrance and managed with a little help from Becky to get her out of the car and into my arms again. I hip-bumped the car door to shut it, not even attempting to lock it up.

The hospital doors swished open, and I strode to the receptionist, shifting Becky in my arms. "Fucking ex-boyfriend beat the shit out of her."

The receptionist hopped up and hurried from behind her desk. "Here—" She pushed open a door and led me into the nurse triage area. I all but fell into the straight-backed chair, holding Becky tight.

A nurse shuffled in, and I gave a quick explanation of what had happened.

Lips pursed, she listened while taking Becky's temperature and pulse. "Pain on a scale of one to ten?" she gently asked Becky while clicking on the computer.

"Eight...n-nine, maybe?" Becky's brow furrowed as more tears leaked from the corners of her clenched eyes.

I hugged her closer.

"Let's get you in a bed," the nurse said, standing. "Do you need a wheelchair?" she asked me as I stood.

"I'll carry her."

Nothing but a hanging sheet separated the bed I laid Becky on and the neighboring person moaning in misery on the other side.

I stepped back, hands clenched, my guts a riotous mess of burning rage.

The nurse pulled back the comforter from Becky's torso. "God," she whispered, gaze trailing over Becky's chest and the dozen or so cane welts, a couple of which oozed blood. She grabbed the blood pressure cuff, ignoring my presence.

A doctor appeared at my elbow, and I forced myself to take a step back and give them room to work.

He looked her over, asking questions—getting the gist of the story he could from her shivering body. The female nurse started an IV while I filled in the blanks for the doctor. While tending to the bleeding welts on her thighs, he asked if we'd called the cops.

I told him we hadn't a moment to spare, that all I'd cared about was removing her from the abuser's house without delay.

Hooked up to fluids, wounds tended to, and waiting for the police to arrive, Becky lay pale and unmoving.

Once the doctor and nurse left us, I pulled a chair forward and sat beside her, brushing dark strands of hair behind her ears.

She shifted her face toward me, and I cupped her uninjured cheek, allowing myself to finally breathe.

My body finally settled, and I sagged against the hardbacked chair, drained. My chest ached, and I wanted nothing more than to wrap Becky up in my arms and hold her to me. Block out the memories of her last twelve years up to that moment. Fill her mind and heart with laughter and light. I leaned forward and kissed her brow, nose, and cheek.

"D-don't leave me," she whispered, eyes still closed.

"Never," I promised before gently brushing my lips across hers.

ℱℰ

It wasn't until two in the morning that they released Becky into my care. Welts, bruises, and a few lacerations along with a slight concussion...shit could have been a hell of a lot worse.

She decided to press charges.

Personally, I wanted the fucker shot as did her cousin who I'd taken a few minutes to finally update. She'd cursed me out for waiting so fucking long—for silencing my cell so I hadn't even been aware she'd been attempting to get in touch with me for hours.

I felt like an asshole, Chantelle labeled me as such, but I knew once shit calmed down, we would be good again.

Cops had asked a million questions. Paperwork required my signature since Becky couldn't grip a pen. Exhaustion lay heavy on both our shoulders by the time I got us into my house and up the stairs to my bedroom.

Becky passed out on my mattress, the skin between her brows unlined, face relaxed in sleep aided by some heavy-duty medication.

I stripped out of my clothes and crawled under the blankets beside her, keeping my body away from her bruised and battered form. Threading my fingers through hers, I brushed my lips over her forehead. "Sleep, sweetness. Rest and don't worry about anything. I'll be here."

Her lips parted with a sigh as though she'd heard me.

I relaxed my head onto the pillow to watch her sleep, determined to watch over her through the night.

Chapter 24

Becky

Daniel roused me from sleep every two hours like he'd been instructed to do, blessedly tearing me from haunting dreams every single time.

I'd been able to do little more than stagger along behind Stephen as he had pulled me from the car and into his house after abducting me. Dizzy, confused, and unstable, I hadn't thought to fight or cry out for help.

God knew he didn't have Daniel's strength to lift and carry me down the stairs into the playroom. Had I gone willingly? I couldn't remember through the fog in my brain

I hadn't fought when he'd ripped my work clothes off of me. Couldn't focus on his face as he had stretched my arms and legs out, tying me tight to the cross. I'd turned my head as he tried to shove the ball gag between my lips, and he'd clobbered me on the bruised cheek again. Darkness had crept in for a second time.

The first strike of the cane had brought reality back with a mean bite, jerking me in my restraints. I'd shrieked, but his curses, his calling me a whore, overshadowed my voice.

He had lashed out in his raging madness over and over again until I could do nothing more than sag and whimper, my throat raw and aching, tears and snot running with abandon.

Panting, he had taken a break, leaving me in the cold room with the lights off, in and out of consciousness as candlelight flickered in my periphery creating ghosts—demons—where none lurked.

Twice more, he had used the cane on my body until his arms hung at his sides.

I'd gladly given in to the blackness sucking on my soul when it came calling.

Daniel hollering my name had jolted me awake, to an agony-flooded existence. I'd weakly pulled against the ropes digging into my skin and tried to scream, new tears leaking from the corners of my eyes.

My redheaded angel...

"Becky?" His warm breath caressed my lips as it had a dozen times or so.

"Hmm?" I tried to turn toward his warmth, but pain wracked my body. I winced, returning to consciousness sooner than I wished.

"Here." He lifted my head. "Pills."

I opened my mouth, and he dropped two tablets in. He held a glass of water to my lips, and I drank deeply, swallowing them down.

A sigh shuddered down through me, and I forced my eyelids up. Sunlight filtered through the blinds of his bedroom windows. "Time?" I rasped, my throat still raw from screaming.

"Six. You've been sleeping for fifteen hours. How are you feeling?"

"Sore." I tried for a smile and tilted my head to meet his

gaze for the first time since he'd tumbled down the stairs to rescue me.

A slew of emotions poured from his eyes, and I choked on an unexpected sob.

"Shh." He lay beside me, soothing a hand over my shoulder.

"H-hold me," I said, turning into him, uncaring of the pain all down the front of my body and how moving stretched skin wanting to be left alone.

He gently cradled me to him, and I cried against his rock-hard chest, my tears soaking his T-shirt. His hand trailed down my spine, slow circles and gentle kneads into my flesh as I unleashed a torrent of emotions. It seemed hours that I immersed myself in his comfort while emptying my soul to exhaustion. Peace settled in along with clarity. The medication had worn down a bit, leaving me more lucid.

"There's no better place than in your arms." I finally broke the quietness of his bedroom.

"You don't know how happy I am to hear you say that." His chest rumbled beneath my ear, and even though I ached, warmth grew between my thighs.

I sighed and smiled, breathing in the citrusy scent of his cologne and the male virility clinging to his skin. "You make everything go away," I whispered. "All of the bad. The ugly, until the only thing I can think about is you."

"You're going to swell my head," he murmured against my hair.

"Which one?"

He chuckled and kissed the top of my head. "Both."

"If..." My voice trailed off as I considered the question I wanted to ask him. While I'd spoken with the police at the hospital, I hadn't gone into great detail about everything

Stephen had done to me. Shame for allowing myself to be vulnerable to his actions made me want to curl into a ball and disappear.

But Daniel would never judge me. He knew my heart.

"If I tell you every detail so I can unburden my mind, will you become angry?" I finally asked.

"I won't lie and say no. Even hearing what you shared with the female cop made me want to go find that fucker and bring down justice on his head."

"I-I need to talk about this, Daniel."

He kissed my forehead, a heavy exhale emptying his lungs. "Then don't hold back—I promise I won't go anywhere. I'll stay here and hold you for as long as you need."

"Will you allow the cops to deal with him?"

"Yes," he didn't hesitate to answer. "I got lucky once dishing out justice—I'm not about to tempt fate and remove myself from a future I have high hopes for."

Peace and yet excitement slid over me like a warm breeze.

"I never should have agreed to speak with him," I started. "But I'd been feeling confident from finally taking a stand for myself. Perhaps I thought confronting Stephen and sharing the truth for a change wouldn't be as difficult as I'd always imagined. I'd been nervous and shaky but we needed closure.

"He seemed contrite, and I expected his usual apologies, promises to never do shit like that again, etc. I made an even graver mistake by agreeing to get out of the cold and sit in his car. I told him I was leaving, and he punched me, the whiplash crashing the back of my head against his passenger window."

Daniel lay silent while I spoke, unloading every

memory, every hazy thing I could remember of what had happened. Being restrained. Cursed out. Beaten until unconsciousness had claimed me more times than I'd been able to count.

Stephen had never abused me to the point of blacking out. He'd never drawn blood out of anger. I couldn't remember a time when I recognized he saw me merely as property—not a human being. He'd given me all he had, and his full strength had left me battered and bruised.

My relationship with Stephen was well and truly over. I'd considered that truth two nights earlier while Daniel had loved me, but the truth now lay like a granite slab deep in my heart.

Daniel Cooney was the man I wanted, both body and soul.

A therapist would probably have a shit ton to say about my latching onto my new Sir without question or more caution, but I knew deep inside that we had been meant to meet that night in my cousin's club.

I would have to get in touch with Chantelle even though Daniel informed me he'd kept her up to date on what had happened.

But she could wait along with the rest of the world.

Daniel continued to hold me long after I fell silent. Tension radiated off him, but he didn't leave my side, nor did his strong hands stop caressing me. Eventually, he relaxed, and we lay silent.

It would be days before I felt well enough to go back to work—

"Shit," I muttered, attempting to pull away from Daniel.

"What?"

"I have to call my boss—"

"I already took care of it," he murmured, shifting me so I

rested on my back. He propped up on an elbow, dark eyes scanning my features.

"How bad is it?" I whispered, watching the war of anger and empathy take place across the battlefield of his face.

"Bad enough that any woman experiencing domestic abuse would see you and reconsider returning to the men who claim to love them."

I frowned hard and winced. "Every inch of me aches," I muttered, "and don't let me see a mirror, please. The last thing I need is another reminder of what that asshole did to me."

"No mirrors. Got it." Daniel leaned down and brushed his lips over mine. "But how about coffee? Maybe some food?"

My stomach growled loudly in agreement, causing us both to smile. "I think I can manage to get up—"

"Nope." Daniel pressed a hand to my chest, keeping me still. "Today is a breakfast-in-bed kind of day."

Tears stung my eyes. "I-I've never been served like that before."

"Best get used to it, sweetness," he stated, rolling away from me to climb off his bed. "Because I'm going to spoil you rotten."

"I'm going to gain another fifty pounds," I muttered, having heard all about his enjoyment of cooking the night we'd cuddled after sex and talked long into the morning hours.

"Just more for me to love on," Daniel said.

I snorted but didn't disagree. I kind of liked the idea of my man loving every inch of me—fluff and all.

My man.

God, I loved those two words. Maybe someday I would

ask him to be that. And if he agreed? I would put a ring on his hand...

Maybe *I* ought to leash *him*.

Snickering, I snuggled back into his bed, breathing in the warm scent of him on the pillow cradling my head.

Chapter 25

Daniel

Chantelle showed up that afternoon. She arrived on my doorstep three hours after I'd called her. Becky had needed more rest after eating the pancakes and sausage I'd made for her, and I assured her I would fill her cousin in on what had gone down so she wouldn't have to repeat it yet again.

Fuck knew Becky had relived it enough between the cops and spilling all the sickening details over my ears.

But I'd saved the horror for later, simply telling Chantelle over the phone that she was safe—and wasn't going out of my sight until the cops caught that fucker.

A dozen bags minimum hung off Chantelle's arms when I pulled open my front door.

She breezed past me, heading straight up the stairs as though already aware of my home's layout.

"She's sleeping," I called out quietly, and Chantelle halted halfway up the stairwell.

"Fuck," she grumbled. Turning, she maneuvered the bags making her a few too many inches wide to fit between the wall and railing. Still cursing, she managed to right everything and tread back to the entryway.

Humphing, she dropped her loot. "Vodka?"

"Sure thing." Smirking, I turned and went to the kitchen.

Her heels clacked behind me on the hardwood flooring.

"Looks like you did some shopping," I stated the obvious.

"Well, seeing as how I don't want Becky to have anything—*anything*—from her old life, I had to hit the mall."

I grabbed a bottle of Grey Goose from the freezer and poured us both a healthy splash in tumblers. Chantelle's may have had an extra inch above mine, but she would need it for the story I'd promised to share with her once she arrived.

She kicked the drink back in one gulp then poured herself another.

Eyeing her spiked heels, I suggested we head to the living room. I couldn't imagine having stormed around the mall for her those purchases in a matter of hours.

She sat in my recliner like a queen, tumbler in hand, long legs crossed at the knee, her eyes flint and fire. "Talk. And don't leave out one goddamned detail, or I'll flog your ass until you cry like a newborn."

I held back my snort. Barely. Sipping my ice-cold liquor, I considered the words I had to speak so the woman I loved wouldn't have to.

Knowing her cousin would want to hear it all, I didn't leave out a single detail that had been burned into my memory by Becky's broken voice.

Chantelle seethed, her face flushed. "I'm going to fucking kill him."

"How about you string him up and we can both beat the shit out of him?" I suggested, only half joking.

One of her eyebrows popped up as though she considered my suggestion.

"Daniel?"

I hopped up at Becky's call. Chantelle followed me to the entryway. We both loaded our arms and made our way up the stairs.

Becky sat against the headboard like she had earlier to eat. Some color had returned to her pale face. Although purple darkened her cheekbone and one eye swelled half-shut, she appeared a lot better than before her nap.

"Hey," she murmured at Chantelle.

Her cousin dropped her bags and strode across the bedroom—finally kicking off those goddamned heels in the process. She sat on the bed, legs curled beneath her, studying Becky's bruises.

"I'm going to fucking murder him," she muttered.

"I'd rather see him rot in jail," Becky stated firmly. "You're the only family I have left, so stay on this side of the law, please."

Chantelle made an annoyed snorting noise. "That bastard is lucky I love you."

Becky peeked around her cousin to meet my gaze. "Can you help me into the bathroom? My bladder is about to burst."

We took care of business, then Chantelle began the fashion show, emptying bag after bag.

New clothing piled around Becky, whose eyes had filled with tears. She hadn't had anything new in years—she and Stephen had only ever had enough money for secondhand things.

Lace and satin panties joined the mess, and I cocked an eyebrow at Becky when she glanced at me, flushing.

I stood against the wall, arms crossed and relaxed until that moment. Imagining sliding those panties off her smooth thighs and baring her pretty pussy for my hungry mouth—

Clearing my throat, I offered to head downstairs to make us something to eat.

"I got takeout from Bertonelli's," Chantelle said with a snap of her fingers as though just remembering. "All of your favorites. The bags are in my Beamer if you would be a dear and retrieve them, Daniel?"

Snickering, I did as told.

I had a feeling a lot of orders would be flying around my home in the coming days.

But I was more than okay with that if it meant having Becky beside me. And with Chantelle being her only family, I expected they might be somewhat of a packaged deal.

That, too, I could live with since the Domme had proven herself to be fiercely loyal and as protective as me.

Twenty minutes later, we ate picnic-style in my bedroom, and I learned all about Becky's childhood from Chantelle's perspective rather than the stories Becky had told me a few nights earlier.

By the time Becky needed some meds and more rest, I swore I could paint some of the memories they had shared.

I'd also gotten grilled, the two women were a lethal combination that fucking flayed me alive. Chantelle learned the entire truth of what had happened when I'd been a fearful thirteen-year-old. She'd even gotten tears in her eyes when her lips had pursed.

I also shared about the years spent with my grandpop who, while he wasn't abusive, wasn't exactly kind either.

Shame didn't attempt to choke me out when I told Becky and Chantelle what I'd had to do in order to survive in the streets of Boston when I'd first arrived, damn near penniless with a single backpack over my shoulder.

"Why Boston?" Chantelle asked.

"Far enough away from Spokane to start over and a big enough city with enough opportunities to create a new life."

"I'm glad you came here," Becky said, her voice quiet. "And I hope you know I won't ever judge you for what you did to put food in your belly."

Getting on my knees wasn't something I'd ever been proud of, but I refused to feel shame since I'd survived. Thrived.

When my grandpop passed, a lawyer had somehow tracked me down. By that time, I'd held a steady job for almost five years, had managed to build some credit, and had a couple of college classes under my belt.

The inheritance I'd received as his only living relative wasn't much, but it paid my tuition through graduation.

"And the rest?" I shrugged, studying my dark-haired beauty who appeared on the verge of once more fading into sleep. "Is history."

I lounged in a chair alongside Becky's edge of my bed, pretty much talked out.

"You're one of the most intuitive Doms I've ever met," Chantelle told me what I'd heard a couple of times before. "I'm sorry it took that kind of trauma to bring you to this place. You too," she said, turning toward Becky who slumped on the bed beside her. "I knew the minute I met Daniel that he would be perfect for you."

"You never held a giveaway, did you?" Becky asked, her jaw cracking on a yawn immediately afterward.

"Nope. That was just me being me and attempting to achieve what I wanted."

Becky's light laughter warmed my chest. "You *always* get your way."

Chantelle stared at her cousin as she snuggled into my pillow, her eyes sparkling with glee. "And this is by far the best thing I've ever done if I do say so myself."

Wetness welled in Becky's eyes when she glanced at me. "I'm going to have to agree with you on that one, Chantelle," she murmured. The emotion pouring from her gaze hit me like an axe to the chest.

Me too, sweetness. Me too.

Chapter 26

Becky

Almost a week after the attack, I felt well enough to take a drive to Stephen's house and collect what things I could—with a police escort.

Daniel held my hand as we walked up the crooked front walkway, the police sitting in their cruiser in the driveway.

Stephen had been missing since I'd pressed charges, the house supposedly empty, his car gone. With no job and no money, I couldn't begin to imagine how he survived or where he'd gone. Like me, he had no family to speak of, but I, at least, had found someone who had my back.

My palm sweated against Daniel's, my stomach twisted into knots as we entered the shack I had called home for many years. I stopped in the living room entrance, my gaze flitting over the shattered figurines I'd collected over the years, the smashed desk I had used to pay the bills. Papers scattered over the floor amidst the many paperback novels I had often escaped into.

The kitchen revealed more of the same, my grandmother's old tin pie plates I'd had hanging on the wall as decoration bent in half and tossed on the floor. My mother's glass casserole dish with the yellow flowers lay in pieces beside the sink. My throat tightened as I turned away.

Without uttering a word, I trudged up the stairs, hand still grasping Daniel's in a death grip.

The bedroom mattress had been slashed apart, stuffing ripped out and thrown around the room. He had torn all of my undergarments. Knifed my jeans, shirts, and sweatshirts, and tossed over the floor. My box of old photographs from when I was a kid had been fetched from the top of our closet. The images scattered over the clothing had been X'd out in black Sharpie—forever ruined. Not one picture had escaped his handiwork.

Tears pricked my eyes, but I refused to shed tears. I wouldn't allow Stephen the satisfaction of hurting me yet again with his actions.

For whatever reason, Stephen had left the bathroom alone.

But as with my clothing, Chantelle had insisted on new everything. I eyed my old hairspray, the brush I should have tossed long ago, and hair ties that had lost elasticity due to overuse and age. While I hadn't expected to find anything of mine untouched, I had figured a walk-through would help me gain closure and also prove that I had nothing worthwhile keeping from my past.

Daniel and I made our way back downstairs, having achieved what I'd wanted.

"What about the basement?" Daniel asked quietly.

I shook my head. There was nothing there I wished to see again, nothing that might hold fond memories. Even if there had been, Stephen had proved my things wouldn't have survived.

One of the officers climbed from the squad car as we exited the house empty-handed.

"Thank you," I said, smiling at the gray-haired man, "but I'm afraid we wasted your time. There's nothing left in there for me."

Lips in a thin line, the officer nodded. "If you hear from him or see him, please get in contact with us."

Daniel and I both shook the officer's hand and climbed into his SUV, a huge sigh of relief blowing between my lips and causing me to sag into the leather seat. "I never have to go back there."

"Never." He put the car into drive and reached for my hand.

Smiling, my heart light, I squeezed my fingers around his.

Even though Stephen was still out there somewhere doing who the hell knew what, I couldn't have been more peaceful. Happy. I finally understood the saying "free as a bird." The sense of relief was almost as euphoric as the afterglow of a climax...almost.

"Want to grab go some lunch?" Daniel asked, removing his hand from mine to flick on the turn signal and take us back onto the on-ramp to the highway.

"Sure." I could always eat no matter my state of mind, and I adored that Daniel didn't care that I didn't watch my caloric intake.

"What are you in the mood for?"

The thought of his ropes and the hardness of his body came to mind, heating my face.

He cast a sideways glance my way when I didn't answer. Chuckling, he turned his focus on the road and merged into fast-moving traffic. "While I would love to fulfill whatever fantasy is running through your mind right now," he murmured, his voice low, "you had a single piece of toast for breakfast."

"I was thinking—"

"What the fuck!"

Something slammed into my side of the car, and I grabbed hold of the dashboard as Daniel grasped the steering wheel steady. Heart in my throat, I glanced out the passenger window.

Stephen glowered at me from inside his old car. Face mottled—eyes red-rimmed.

Drunk and deep in a rage—

"Look out!" I shrieked as he jerked the wheel and smashed the side of his car into Daniel's again.

"Call 911," Daniel said, swerving into another lane and putting some distance between Stephen and us.

I grabbed his phone from the console, my hands shaking. A woman's voice came over the line, and I started to tell her our emergency.

"Fuck!" Daniel bit out the curse as Stephen drove into the back corner of the SUV before getting behind us. He stayed on the bumper, and Daniel fought to keep the car straight.

Hemmed in on all sides in the middle of the highway, we had nowhere to go.

Half-hysterical, I blubbered into the cell phone, trying to tell the woman what was happening, my head whipping around, trying to keep track of Stephen's clunker as slowing traffic allowed him to continue battering the SUV.

"Where are you? What mile marker?" she asked, her voice calm.

"I-I don't—" I peered ahead, and Daniel sped up as traffic allowed, swerving into the right lane.

Stephen smashed into the driver's side, and I shrieked, grabbing hold of the dashboard. Eyes wide and filled with madness, he met my gaze across Daniel's body. He dragged a finger over his throat while drifting toward our left.

"Hold on!" Daniel stomped on the brakes as Stephen yanked his steering wheel our way.

The front of Daniel's car clipped the rear fender of Stephen's, sliding him sideways.

I blinked.

The undercarriage of Stephen's car filled our windshield and flipped before I realized what had happened. Pieces of plastic and metal scattered as we slowed, a few other cars skidding off the highway to avoid Stephen's tumbling car.

We stopped along with dozens of other vehicles.

Sounds of rear-ending cars behind us sounded in the sudden silence.

My heart thudded in my ears as I clutched the cell in my hand, fighting for breath.

"Are you okay?" Daniel's rumbling voice seemed far away as the woman on the phone spewed questions. "Becky."

I jerked my gaze off the mangled car resting on its roof in the middle of the highway.

Daniel cupped my cheek in his hand. "Okay?" he repeated

"Y-yes."

"Stay here."

I nodded and realized the 911 operator was still trying to get my attention. "Th-there's been an accident..."

My focus went to Daniel as he strode toward Stephen's car, but I answered the woman's questions.

"Help is on the way," she said.

I hung up and lifted my gaze to Daniel. He rounded the car and pulled up short, hands raised.

No, no, no!

Someone knocked on the passenger window, and I shrieked, shying away.

A middle-aged woman waved. "Are you alright?" she asked, her voice muffled through the window.

I shot my gaze back toward Daniel. He hadn't shifted from his stance, but his mouth moved.

A man entered my periphery on the right, stalking forward, gun in hand and held in front of his body like a police officer even though he wore jeans and a T-shirt. He crept around the back of Stephen's car.

"Drop it!" I heard him holler—and all hell broke loose.

Gunshots erupted, making me scream again.

Daniel spun and fell to the ground.

"No!" I screamed and fumbled to open the door.

The kind woman hunkered behind the car beside me, hands over her ears, but I couldn't spare her a second glance.

"Daniel!" I cried out, the ache in my chest attempting to pull me to the ground.

Daniel pushed up onto his knees, and I released a sob.

He glanced my way—back to Stephen behind his car— to me again. He held up his hand, asking me to stay put.

I halted my stumbling steps toward him, shaking my head. Shivering. On the verge of vomiting.

My ears rang as I went light-headed.

Breathe...

I sucked oxygen into my lungs. "D-Daniel..." I sputtered, barely putting tone to my single word.

He mumbled something to the gunman who'd stepped behind Stephen's overturned vehicle. I could make out the top of his dark head.

Sirens sounded in the distance.

Daniel turned toward me—blood covered his left shoulder.

I swallowed hard, my legs going weak. The ground came up to meet me, but Daniel got to me first, his strong arms slowly lowering me to a sitting position.

"Head between your knees, sweetness," he murmured, his voice steady. "The bullet barely grazed me—I'm fine."

Struggling to breathe, I did as told, clutching at his hand. Warm. Calloused. Real—alive.

"S-Stephen?" I gasped out.

"Dead." No hint of remorse lined his answer.

Nothing but relief swept through me, and I stared at the road beneath us, dry-eyed and silent.

Daniel wrapped his arms around me, clutching me close as emotion swamped my brain, filling my ears with loud static...like too many thoughts and feelings crowded in, fighting for dominance. I ignored everything. Chose the numbness of keeping the shit away. Nothing could hurt me —I wouldn't have to face the truth of everything I'd experienced, all I had lived through, the previous handful of years.

I found peace that morning as sirens blared and voices hollered. Quietness in a way that helped me cope with what I didn't want to face.

Chapter 27

Daniel

The man who had shot Stephen was an FBI agent headed to his Boston office. Had it not been for him being late that morning, I would have been the one hauled off in a black bag rather than Becky's ex.

Stephen had been hurt badly when his car rolled, his body half-out of the driver's window, leg pinned beneath metal and plastic. Blood had covered his head, filled his mouth so his teeth stained crimson when he'd pulled his gun on me and promised to watch me bleed out.

I'd seen the agent approaching in my periphery and watched him round the backside of Stephen's car. I'd managed to keep Stephen talking rather than taking me out by stating that Becky was his—always would be. She missed him. Wanted to spend the rest of her life submitting to him.

A pile of fucking lies, but it was what the bastard had needed to hear at that moment so he wouldn't pull the goddamn trigger.

The officer had made a scuffling noise behind Stephen before hollering for him to drop his gun.

Dual shots had rung out, and fire had ripped over my shoulder, spinning me around and to the ground.

Teeth gritted, I'd stayed put until Becky called out to me, her voice ragged. Overwhelmed by emotion. On the edge of losing her shit.

A glance was all it had taken for me to know Stephen wouldn't look her way again.

I'd gone to her. Held her. Assured her I would be fine—which I was.

Stephen's bullet had only grazed my left shoulder, enough to bleed but not require stitches. I was patched up by an EMT onsite, refusing to go to the hospital.

Traffic had backed up for miles behind us, and I'd never been so thankful for life. The ability to fill my lungs. Luck allowing no other vehicle to be involved in Stephen's rage and eventual wreck. Becky clinging to me for days afterward, refusing to leave my side, her hands greedy, her body insatiable with need.

No matter my physical assurance of health, desire for her, or the love I lavished on her, she rode an edge of anxiety, refusing to find release. She'd emptied her well of tears, but something held her mind prisoner. She slept well. Ate whatever I put in front of her and then some. But she took no pleasure from our interactions.

Chantelle visited, and I gave the two women space, heading over to Micah's Sunday afternoon for the Sox game.

Only Jarod joined us, and I sucked down two beers while filling them both in on what had happened.

"How's Becky doing?" Jarod asked, his dark eyes intense and knowing. He'd faced death with Christine and had probably experienced similar PTSD or whatever it was that haunted Becky about the terrifying afternoon of Stephen's death.

"She's going through the motions but isn't living," I replied. "Not really. Won't discuss what happened—in their torn apart house or anything after that morning we left it behind for good. It's like she's shut herself down."

And I felt powerless to help bring her back to life.

"Give her some time," Micah suggested. "She's been through some serious shit. I can't imagine she'll be ready to move on from that sort of trauma like the flip of a light switch."

"Maybe take her to see a therapist?" Jarod said, shifting forward on the couch to rest his elbows on his knees while he angled to face me. "Christine and I have been seeing someone once a month, both by ourselves and as a couple. I'll be honest —I always thought shrinks were for the weak, but I've learned better ways of thinking. Communicating. How to allow my emotions their place. I'm telling you, it's so damn worth it."

I contemplated Jarod's words, having already considered suggesting a therapist once Becky settled a bit. But maybe waiting wasn't the answer. Perhaps she needed a figurative slap to the face. But what? And how? Real talk hadn't accomplished shit. Asking her to share her thoughts and feelings with me earned me nothing but a dismissive smile and an *I'm fine*.

"Set her free."

My head jerked toward Micah, a scowl denting my forehead. "No fucking way."

He barked a laugh, his blue eyes twinkling. "Not like that you fuckhead—string her ass up. Take her out of her mind and send her soaring. Isn't that what you do with your ropes? Same as I do when inflicting desired pain?"

"Fuck." I slumped back on his couch, scrubbing a hand down over my face. Could it be that simple? Asking her to submit to me, entice her to trust me with her body, her mind? She fell so easily those first two times...

The more I considered it, the more I realized I'd had the power to break through her block all along.

I hopped up, drawing both men's gazes. "Gotta go."

Neither questioned me as I spun on my heel and headed toward the entryway.

"Good luck!" Micah called out.

I expected I would need it regardless of my absurdity in being able to give Becky what she needed. What her body craved. What her soul required to find her footing once more so she could face forward and begin living her second chance at life.

Chantelle climbed into her Beamer in front of my house when I pulled into the driveway. She rolled down her window as I approached.

"How is she?" I asked.

"Claims to be fine, but she isn't." Chantelle glanced over at my front door. "She has to talk to someone. A mental health professional or something, because I can't get through to her."

"Do you think she's grieving Stephen?" I asked the question that had haunted me since I'd told Becky he was dead.

Chantelle snorted. "Fuck no. She's glad he's gone. Vehemently told me so with enough curses to make my ears ring."

"Then what the fuck, Chantelle?" I pulled at my hair, frustrated as fuck. "She won't share anything with me. Won't tell me what's going on in her head."

"Then take her out of it since I'm unable to do so."

I nodded, not surprised Chantelle and Micah would be on the same page. Huffing a heavy exhale, I eyed my house as though I could see Becky inside, use X-ray vision to seek out her emotional status through brick and mortar.

"Using your ropes won't heal whatever is affecting her thought processes and shutting her down, but it will definitely crack the walls cutting her off from you. Baby steps, Daniel. Use your intuition. Poke and pry with determined persistence. You're one of the best I've ever seen. Trust yourself. Your instincts."

My throat tightened as Chantelle's words settled over me. She spoke of more than my being a Dom...

"Thank you," I croaked.

Chantelle smiled up at me from her driver's seat. "I'm simply telling you the truth, Daniel. Now go in there, tie my cousin up, and quiet her mind. Love on her body and mind until she remembers what it feels like to live again."

Teeth gritted, I nodded.

The engine of Chantelle's Beamer faded in the distance while I studied the front of my house. My home. The life I'd built from nothing. The future I hoped to share with a healed Becky by my side.

Mind set on getting exactly what I wanted, I strode forward, refusing to be swayed.

Becky might have the power while sceneing, but I was going to remind her what it felt like to be free. Satiated. Peaceful in mind and spirit.

I wouldn't be denied.

Somehow, some way, I would send Becky to the stars. Lighten her burdens then bring her safely back to the reality she didn't need to fear facing. I would assure her of my support. My loyalty.

My love.

Nothing would stand as a barrier against me, especially a fucking corpse rotting six feet under. I wouldn't allow him to have power over Becky's and my relationship. The fucker was dead. Couldn't touch her—*wouldn't* ever touch her again.

Becky belonged to me, and it was about time I took care of my woman in the best way I knew how.

Chapter 28

Becky

I curled up on Daniel's bed, dry-eyed and staring at the bureau across the room. The numbness that had settled over me on the day Stephen had died remained, a heavy, comforting blanket of quietness.

Chantelle had tried to rile me up. Hollered and bitched at me to get some sort of emotional reaction out of me. She'd failed, same as Daniel's quiet insistence to share my heart with him. I didn't want to talk about Stephen. Didn't want to even think about the years I'd wasted on his ass. Didn't want to face the fact I'd allowed myself to be abused—tortured both physically and emotionally—for years.

I had chosen him.

I had stayed regardless of the pain.

I had submitted in hopes of helping him heal.

And I hated myself for those three truths.

Muttering beneath my breath, I shoved all that shit back into the box in a corner of my mind.

"Becky?" Daniel called from downstairs, but I didn't have the energy to respond.

Chantelle had dragged shit up I hadn't wanted to discuss. She'd exhausted me.

Heavy footfalls I recognized announced Daniel's climbing of the stairs. I listened as he traversed the hardwood flooring in the hallway. Awareness of him skittered down my spine, but I tamped the beginnings of desire away, self-loathing too damned strong to allow me enjoyment of anything.

I could feel his eyes on me but didn't roll to face him.

He approached, my skin itching to acknowledge him.

Eyes closing, I squashed the yearning for him down deep where it wouldn't be roused.

Daniel rounded the foot of the bed. The bottom drawer of the dresser squeaked, and my heart rate kicked up at the memory of what he kept there. Regardless of my need to keep a tight rein on my body, craving lit in my core.

"Becky." He sounded close—too fucking close.

I couldn't find my voice.

"Do you remember your safeword, sweetness?"

Oh, God. I gulped, his low tone making goose bumps rise along my skin. Every cell giving me life tingled, refusing to be stuffed in the corner of safety I'd created for myself.

I didn't want to feel. Didn't want to think. Didn't want to lose my shit—

"Stand up. Face me, eyes on the floor."

As though Daniel commanded my mind, I slid off the edge of the mattress without hesitation. Even though I knew he would never hurt me physically, I cowered before him, my focus on the navy blue rug beneath my bare feet.

Rather than tipping my chin up as I expected, Daniel stayed put, feet in a wide stance. "Strip."

My hands moved on autopilot, pulling my T-shirt off overhead. I unclasped my bra, allowing it to fall to the floor and leaving my large breasts unbound and sagging. The linen sleep pants Chantelle had gifted me slipped soundless down around my ankles once untied from my waist.

Skin once more pebbling, I shivered...unsure if it was due to want—both physically and to escape where my emotions couldn't be flayed open.

"Panties too."

An audible swallow worked my throat as I did as told.

"Good girl," Daniel murmured.

I closed my eyes, my breath leaving in a rush at his simple words of edification. I'd made the right choice...had listened to his commands. Although broken parts of me wanted to hide, my subconscious insisted on doing what was right—necessary to move on.

Even in his death, Stephen had somehow spelled me into submission to his darkness, the complete hindrance of anything positive in my life. But I was done with the man. He, along with all the memories of our many years together, needed to be shoved in that goddamned box in my head keeping me from a better future.

The numbness broke me apart at the seams, unraveling...leaving me shaking.

"Becky?" Daniel checked in with me, his voice full of concern.

"Green, Sir," I rasped out, on the verge of breaking.

"Do I have permission to touch you?"

Throat thickening, I nodded, a desperate ache for him settling in my chest. "Yes—Master Cooney."

A low groan escaped his lips and swept warmth through my core, giving me something delicious to focus on.

Arousal—blessed *need* pulsed to life inside me.

I whimpered with want as he stepped in closer, filling

my vision with his jean-clad legs and the massive bulge between his thighs.

My mouth watered, and I dug my fingernails into my palms to keep from reaching for him. I shifted on my feet, my pulse kicking up a notch as I grew damp between my thighs.

He traced his fingertips down my cheeks, my neck, over the swell of my breasts, my nipples hardening to points.

My entire focus zoomed in on his gentle touch. Every caress over skin that grew needier by the minute. He splayed his hand over my soft belly before mapping upward once more to my shoulder. Down my arm. To my wrist, which he grasped.

"I'm going to use my ropes on you."

"Yes, Sir," I willingly agreed, remembering what he could offer me—how I had the power to take what I wanted or shut him down if I grew uncomfortable.

I wouldn't.

Nothing about Daniel threatened me in any way. He was my safe place. My home.

He led me to the foot of his bed, and in silence, he began wrapping me in a chest harness.

I closed my eyes, submitting to the light touches of his hands and rope, moving with him as he bound my torso. My heavy breasts hung free, but he tied my hands behind me at my lower back without discomfort.

Breaths shallow, I rested, my mind buzzing—alive and yet still at the same time. I sank into the peaceful feeling, yearning for more. His touch.

"Facedown on the bed, sweetness," he whispered against my ear, the scrape of his scruff sending a shiver down my spine.

I did as told, and he bound my ankles to the backs of my

thighs, connecting the ropes to the harness above my hands near the middle of my spine. My inhales remained quiet, although need still throbbed in my core.

Daniel stepped away, and I floated on the edge of reality, barely aware of his movements.

Anticipation a live wire under my skin, I waited for him to string me up to one of the massive hooks he had in his bedroom ceiling. I'd seen the pulley system, just never in action.

A warm palm slid up my shin toward my ankle. Over my limp hands. He grasped the harness, more gentle tugs nudged my body as he once more tied knots.

"I'm going to suspend you," Daniel said in his rumbling voice, and a moan rose from my chest.

Whispered footsteps sounded—and a slow pull hefted me into the air.

My head hung relaxed, breasts swinging, the harness at my lower back distributing my weight along the loops and knots wrapped around my body. I envisioned the ropes as his hands, holding me, caressing me, and keeping me in his care.

I'd never felt as safe as I did in that moment. Nothing mattered but the bindings around me and the sense of security they offered.

"You look so beautiful," he said, running his hands along my legs, squeezing and kneading my flesh between the loops cradling my limbs. "I've wanted you like this for so long...I don't know how much longer I can wait."

"Please..." My whisper sounded from far off, an echoing in the placid quietness Master Cooney had gifted me.

He spun me in the air and stepped between my spread thighs, sliding a finger down through my ass crack, through my swelled labia, to my clit. "You're exquisite, Becky—how you respond to me. Fucking beautiful."

I moaned, trying to press into his touch, but couldn't move. Completely at his mercy, I whimpered, unable to voice my need or even explain how he made me feel.

He fingered around my pussy, barely dipping the tip of his index into me. "So wet," he murmured. "May I taste you, sweet girl?"

My head hung low—I couldn't even nod.

Master Cooney grasped my hip bones and lifted me higher to his mouth. His tongue shoved into my pussy, curling and lapping, his growl of appreciation creating more wetness for him to taste. Arousal, thick and heady, ruled my thoughts. My body. I existed for my Sir's pleasure, nothing else. No memories of the past, trauma, or unhappiness dragged me downward into a spiral. I floated in the air. Desire. On the edge of euphoria.

My core throbbed, and every groan against my pussy lips amped my pulse even as my mind traveled to an even deeper place of rest.

Sir's strong hands lowered me until I was once more suspended by his loving ropes alone. He crowded in close, rubbing the tip of his cock all over my lower lips. "May I have you, Becky?"

I managed to find my voice but could only hum approval. My tongue refused to form words.

He notched. Grasped my hips. Pulled me back onto his steel-like length, filling me in one slow movement.

A guttural whimper leaked past my parted lips, and I panted, brain buzzing, skin prickling.

"You are so perfect for me, sweetness," he said, his voice sending delicious shivers sliding down my spine. He pushed me away and pulled me back onto him again, the tip of him hitting my cervix and making me moan again. "Curves to hold onto, softness and silky heat that drives me insane..."

My breasts began to sway with slow rhythm as he impaled me on every backward swing. He held me gently though his thrusting intensified, hands cradling my body parts like I was a fragile vase. I hovered on the edge, ready to fly and tumble into pure ecstasy I'd tasted while bound once before.

"You're mine," he said, reaching around my waist to brush his fingers over my clit.

I whimpered in agreement.

"Forever." He flicked, and I gasped. "Always."

Tingles came to life in my toes, sweeping up my bound legs and into my stomach.

Daniel pressed in deep and paused, our quickened breaths loud in the quiet room. "I love you, Becky."

Tears welled in my eyes, and a sob exploded from my chest as a torrent of emotion released.

He held still inside me, hands caressing every inch of my skin as I cried the pent up tears I'd stifled for too long.

"Color, sweetness?" he murmured above my sniffles.

"G-Green," I managed to sputter.

"Let it all go," he crooned, cradling my breasts in his strong hands. "I have you."

He backed out of my pussy—and thrust back in.

My climax exploded like stars behind my leaking eyes, tumbling me into ecstasy, seeming to wipe out every hidden hurt, every dark thought until all that existed was Sir. His hands holding me. His cock throbbing against my cervix. His seed flooding me—marking me.

"Fuck, do I love you. So fucking much," he growled, his voice barely heard past the rushing in my ears.

I came again, crying out before going limp in his ropes,

gentle light carrying me away into oblivion where tears didn't exist.

⅊

Soft touches caressed my face. My breasts. My stomach.

"Becky?" Daniel whispered in my ear, stirring my hair.

"Mmm." I stretched, smiling at the soft mattress beneath me and the hard body cradling my right side.

He trailed his fingertips over my stomach. "You should see all the indents in your skin from my ropes, sweetness. So fucking beautiful."

I forced my eyes open and barely managed to lift my head. Marks from the hemp rope Daniel had strung me up with crisscrossed over my torso and stomach, hiding the lingering scars from Stephen's cane.

Love overshadowed the damage from my past.

My throat tightened at the metaphorical image in my mind. Daniel had been my first in so many ways—and he would be my last. I cupped his face in my palm, rubbing my thumb over the red scruff on his chin.

"I love you, Daniel." I kissed his lips, peaceful emotion welling up inside me. "Forever. Always."

He slid his tongue along the seam of my mouth, and I opened, giving over to him...to his tender control and undemanding affection.

Chapter 29

Daniel

Two Years Later

We didn't have an easy journey. No rainbows and unicorns frolicked around us as we traveled together, hand in hand. Becky walked beside me, but I often ended up carrying her. Prompting her forward with gentle nudges. Tied her up when her mind got the best of her.

She agreed to go to counseling, and I sometimes went with her.

Slowly—so fucking slowly—she learned how to accept the choices of her past. Take life lessons from them. Some nights, dreams woke her. Others, I was the one jolted from sleep by memories I wished would remain buried. But we had each other to cling to. Loving arms to hold us, willing ears to listen, encouraging lips to help keep us grounded.

Becky had stayed with me, in my home, without discussion or even prompting. She never suggested she ought to live life on her own for a while. Chantelle, however, *had*, but I put my foot down. No way in hell would I allow Becky to leave my bed.

But my possessiveness ran on the side of protective and nurturing, not assholery.

Eventually, Chantelle stopped her meddling and allowed Becky and I space to grow together.

And grow, we did.

Elite became a thing of my past, and although my friendship with the guys didn't waver and we still got together on the weekends for sports games, I looked forward to returning home to my sweet girl.

The first night I talked Becky into going to Chantelle's club with me, we ended up in a private room where tears flowed. I'd had to string my love up to quiet her spirit, and as with every time I bound her, she settled and found clarity.

Eventually, Chantelle's club became our favorite date place, and Becky's confidence grew to the point she asked me to demonstrate to the club how beautiful bondage could be.

She stared up at me, her dark, clear eyes full of warmth and fervent love that made my chest ache. Hemp weaved around her wrists and torso, but she stood relaxed in her pale purple bikini rather than naked, her breaths even.

A corner of my lip curled at the gorgeous sight of her beauty, and I leaned down, unable to keep from brushing my mouth over hers. "So fucking proud of you, sweetness."

Her radiant smile caused goose bumps to ripple over my flesh and sent blood rushing to my dick.

Uncaring my leathers didn't hide what Becky did to me, I continued with the demonstration in Chantelle's lounge, allowing the patrons a glimpse of what they could accomplish given enough time and practice.

I bound my love, intentionally touching her in spots that

would hinder her from floating fully away to her favorite place. I also kept her arms free.

A simple rigging lifted her off the ground in a seated position but only high enough that when I dropped to my knees in front of her spread thighs, she rested at a level necessary for what I had planned. Most Doms would have bought her a collar, but I refused to ask Becky to wear what Stephen had demanded of her.

More than one gasping patron realized what I was doing before my lover did.

Slipping a ring from my front pocket, I took her left hand.

She blinked, realization dawning on her face. Eyes widening, she glanced from the ring between two of my fingers to my eyes. "Sir," she croaked.

"You are the greatest gift a man could ever wish for," I began, my voice unsteady, throat tight. "If God existed, I would declare she had me in mind while creating every perfect inch of you."

Tears welled in Becky's eyes, quickly spilling down her cheeks. Her breath hitched, jiggling her plump breasts.

"We've had one hell of a trip so far," I continued, "and I wouldn't want anyone else beside me. You're my loyal cheerleader, the light in my darkness, the one I look forward to seeing at the end of a long day. Sweetly submissive with a backbone of steel born by heartache and trauma."

My voice broke, and I swallowed hard as Becky cried silent tears.

"I often go all possessive in claiming you as mine, but the power belongs to you—it has *always* been yours. So here I am on my knees, showing every person here that you own my heart. My soul. This ring is no leash but a representation of unending love, and I'm asking you to wear it. Be mine forever. Walk alongside me through the rest of our lives."

"Yes, Daniel," Becky whispered my real name, and I blinked back tears.

"Sweetness," I rasped out while sliding the ring onto her finger.

She grabbed hold of my face, and I lifted higher to give her my mouth.

While I wanted to bury my aching dick between her thighs, we hadn't yet crossed the line of sharing that part of our relationship with the public. Neither of us got off on exhibitionism, but Becky trusted me with sending her into subspace in front of an audience. Especially since others learned how to do the same for their submissives.

I took my time untying my love, my heart full and my groin throbbing. Thankful as fuck Chantelle had been in on my plans, I couldn't wait to escape to the private room she'd gifted me for the rest of the night.

The second I shut the door behind us, I took Becky in my arms and simply held her. Breathed in the sweet scent of her, soaking in the warmth of her exhales over my chest. Chin rested atop her head, I closed my eyes and allowed myself to simply exist with her. Appreciate every second she gifted me of her time and attention.

Eventually, she grew restless, and I stepped back.

Becky wound one hand behind my neck and tugged while pressing into me, her breasts and belly soft against my skin. "I love you, Daniel Cooney." She gave me her mouth, and I groaned at the feel of her tongue sliding over mine.

My pulse raced, and my balls ached with the need to find release deep inside her.

"Need you," I whispered against the pillow of her lips,

so goddamn ready to sink into her slick heat that my body shook.

"I'm all yours, Sir."

"Nuh uh, none of that. Right now, I'm Daniel, and you're my fiancée, the love of my life." I swung her up into my arms.

She squealed and clutched at me, smacking my shoulder. "You'll throw your back out."

"The fuck I will," I muttered, striding toward the king-sized bed against the wall.

I laid her down, climbing onto the bed atop her on my hands and knees. "Will you ride me, sweetness?"

Her lips pursed, and I expected the answer she'd given me dozens of times before.

"Please," I begged. "I want to be free to touch every inch of your flesh. Your beautiful curves. Want to watch your gorgeous tits bounce while you grind on me. Want your cum to leak all over my balls."

"God." Becky laughed, her cheeks flushing.

I fell off her and grabbed hold of my aching length, holding it upright. "Come on, be a good girl and ride my dick."

"This is so damn embarrassing," she muttered while sitting and swinging one of her legs over my body to straddle me.

"Mmm." I grasped her thick thighs, rubbing and kneading her lush flesh. "Fucking love every inch of you. You're so goddamned delicious."

She rolled her eyes.

"Lift up, baby."

Becky went to her knees, and I shifted, getting the head of my dick where I wanted it.

"I'm all yours," I whispered, giving her the reins, complete control.

She splayed her hands on my pecs. Pink still flushed her cheekbones, but desire and love overcame the uncertainty in her eyes. Our gazes stayed locked, our spirits one, as she sank onto my length.

A deep groan rumbled in my chest as her wet heat engulfed every inch of me. "Fuck, Becky," I rasped through clenched teeth. I'd been worked up for days thinking about getting that rock on her hand, finally having a witness and physical evidence of who owned my heart.

My length throbbed deep inside her, my balls already tight against my groin.

"I'm so fucking close already," I warned her. "Please make my fantasy come to life—please move on me, sweetness."

She shifted forward, dragging her clit over my pelvis, and my abs tightened, hips lifting on instinct to stay buried inside her.

"Fuck." I swallowed hard, grasping at her hips, fighting for control over my instinct to take over.

Another swivel of her hips swayed her tits, and I shifted up to mouth at her soft flesh.

"Oh, God," she whispered and lifted her heavy breast, diamond glittering as she fed me her furled nipple.

I moaned, suckling—and she began to rock atop me, using my dick to give herself pleasure.

Propped on an elbow, I held myself upright so I could continue loving on her tight nub, knowing every suck, every nibble sent shock waves straight to her clit.

Becky grabbed hold of my head, keeping me close. "I'm going to come—Daniel..."

I popped off her nipple and shoved my tongue into her

mouth, stealing her breath and swallowing her cry as she came. Wet heat creamed all over my groin, and I groaned, feet planted on the mattress to fuck up into her spasming pussy.

Fucking. Hell.

She was divine. Lush. Perfect—

My balls detonated, pulsing cum deep against her womb. "Jesus—Becky...fuck, sweetness." I gulped, another spurt clenching every muscle in my body. "Love you so fucking much."

She went limp atop me, and I gave one last shuddered dribble into her tight sheath before going lax.

"Fuck," I grunted, cradling her in my arms.

Her face buried in my neck, her panted breaths hot against my already heated skin.

"So good," I murmured, smoothing my hands down her back to grab her ass. I jiggled her cheeks before hugging her tight. "Won't ever get enough of you," I murmured.

Becky sighed and allowed me to hold her full weight without complaint or embarrassment. "Good thing you put a ring on it, then, huh?"

I huffed a snort and shoved my semi deeper into her wetness. "You're so much more than an it," I told her, shifting my head to the side so I could see her face.

Dark eyes sated, she smiled at me.

"You're my everything. My entire life, Becky Eaton."

"Soon to be Cooney," she corrected me, her soft palm on my scruffy cheek.

"You'll take my last name?" I hadn't expected her to, figuring she would want to hold onto one part of herself once we married.

"If I'm going to belong to the world's most gracious Dom, then I want everyone to know it."

She would give me everything…

"Love you," I whispered, tangling my fist in her hair and pulling her forward to my mouth.

"Love you more," she claimed before I kissed her.

Let her think what she wanted.

I was damned well aware of the truth. No man felt what I did in the center of my being. She owned me, heart and soul, gifting me her body, her submission, and her love in return.

THE END

About the Author

USA Today bestselling author Lynn Burke is a CrossFit and coffee addict. Her three spawn and two fur babies dictate how often she can be found hunched over her Mac, typing as fast as her fickle muse cooks up hot stories.

You can find more about Lynn at her website: www. authorlynnburke.com

Also By Lynn Burke

Abel's Obsession

Divulging Secrets

Healing Storms

In Between

Reluctant Lumberjack

Resisting his Mate

Billion Dollar Love Anthology

Blood Born Series

Bonds of Worship Series

Dark Leopards MC

Darkest Desires Series

Devil's Outlaws MC

Elite Escort Series

Elite Escorts MM Series

Fallen Gliders MC

Forbidden Obsession Duet

Found by Fate Series

Midnight Sun Series

Missing Link Series

Risso Family Series

Sandy Ridge Series

Sinful Nature Series

Vicious Vipers MC

9 781955 635448